# *Picture Me Falling in Love*

We looked at each other, and the river breeze that pushed my hair back, pushed his forward. I wanted to touch those dark curls. I did. Then, almost in slow motion, we leaned toward each other and kissed. My first kiss. My first love.

"Alexandra," Heracles said, "what I've been trying to tell you is, I already have a girlfriend."

JUNE FOLEY

# *Picture Me Falling in Love*

Methuen

To my sisters and brother:
Pat, Nora, Kate, and Kevin;
and our children:
Richard, Dana, Brooke, Jessica,
Christopher, and Max

With special thanks to Marie, Joe,
and Joseph Attanasio; Paula Danziger,
Diana L. Drake, Warren Heiss, Mark Hoffman,
Aaron Kinne, Max Lindenman, and Bobby Stark

First published in the United States 1986
by Delacorte Press under the title
*Falling in Love is No Snap*
This Methuen Teens paperback edition
first published in Great Britain 1988
by Methuen Children's Books Ltd
11 New Fetter Lane, London EC4P 4EE
Copyright © 1986 June Foley
Printed in Great Britain by
Cox & Wyman Ltd, Reading

ISBN 0 416 12022 9

# 1

Shoonck. That was the sound I heard when I first saw Heracles Damaskinakis. It was the sound of the shutter opening and closing as I took my first pictures with my new camera. Actually, it was an old camera—a classy Pantex I found in a secondhand store. Instead of a click or a snap, it made a soft, mellow shoonck.

Shoonck. Shoonck. I shot into the window of the corner deli, trying to get both the old-fashioned inside of the store and the reflection of the sleek, new, high-rise apartments around it. I was already imagining the Museum of Modern Art's future exhibit "Alexandra Susskind's Manhattan."

"Hey, wait a minute." The voice was kind of husky; the words came fast, with a New York accent.

Through the viewfinder I saw a boy stick his head out the deli door. He looked around fifteen—my age. He was tall, slim but broad-shouldered, with dark, curly hair as thick as a mop. He was wearing a long white apron over a Mets sweatshirt, jeans, and sneakers.

With a few long strides the boy came outside, next to the produce display. He grabbed two grapefruit, slipped them under his shirt, one on each shoulder, and posed like a muscleman. "Go ahead," he said.

I laughed, and took more pictures of the deli window. Shoonck. Shoonck. Shoonck.

"Any chance you'll become a great photographer and my father's store will be famous?" the boy asked, putting the grapefruit back in their bin.

"Maybe," I said. "Or maybe I'll become a filmmaker and do a movie about your father's store."

"Make it a science fiction or horror movie." The boy quickly stuck a cabbage under his shirt, on his back, and bent way forward. *The Hunchback of Damaskinakis's Deli*," he said.

I laughed again.

"Or how about a movie about a giant killer sandwich?" the boy said.

"You mean," I said, "instead of a sandwich that people eat, a sandwich that eats people?"

We both cracked up, and I came out from behind my camera. Right away, a stocky man with white hair, dark eyes, and a white mustache stuck his head out the deli door. He yelled at the boy in a foreign language, then went back inside.

"That was Greek for 'Get back to work,'" the boy said, with a wide smile. His teeth were big and white. His eyes were big and brown, with some gold . . . a lot of gold.

Shoonck. Shoonck. Shoonck. I took his picture just before he followed his father.

On the way home I ran into Mom. Actually she ran into me, in her sweatsuit and Nikes, jogging back from her Saturday morning workout in Central Park. "Hi, sweetheart." She slowed down and kissed me on the cheek.

"Mom, can I use the closet in my room as a darkroom and the bathroom to develop my pictures in?" I asked. "And can I have an advance on my next six months allowance to buy film developer, stop bath, fixer, print tongs, timers . . ."

She laughed. "Anything else?"

"The most expensive thing—an enlarger."

"I wish I could say yes," she said, linking her arm in mine as we walked together. "But my salary doesn't do much more than cover our expenses."

"You could send me to public school."

Her short, straight, blond hair swung as she shook her head. "Your school is worth every penny. Your education comes first. You know that."

I knew it, all right. Mom wanted me to go to med school, law school, or the Harvard Business School for a master's in business administration. With her B.A. in liberal arts, she had to start as a secretary after she and Dad got divorced. Now she was managing editor at her textbook publishing company, but it'd taken her years to work her way up while raising me.

Inside our apartment I watched while Mom stood looking through the mail. "Anything from Nora?" I asked. I still thought of Nora Nakamura as my best friend, even though during the summer her father's company had transferred him and the family had moved to Boston.

"Mm . . . not today. . . . Just an L. L. Bean catalog . . . literary magazine . . . bank statement."

"I heard a gross joke about your weird bank, Mom."

"What?"

"The First National Women's Bank closes one week a month—on account of cramps."

Laughing, she bonked me on the head with the mail, then opened the Bean catalog.

"Mom, how old were you when you first met Dad?"

She turned a page before she heard me. "Nineteen," she said, turning to the next page, then looking up. "Why?"

"Just wondering."

"Sweetheart, I've got some work to do." She glanced toward her corner desk. "But we'll eat out tonight . . . the Egyptian restaurant."

I groaned. "What was that stuff I had there—mashed chick-peas with a sauce that looked and smelled like cat food?"

"Falafel," she said.

"Probably because just looking at it makes people feel awful."

"Alexandra . . ." In one second, Mom would go into her "broadening our horizons" speech. "We came to New York to learn and grow," she said. "We're surrounded by every kind of restaurant anybody could imagine . . ."

"And some most people couldn't," I pointed out.

"We'd be foolish not to at least try the cuisines of different countries."

"I've already tried some," I reminded her. "I still prefer the cuisine of my native Nutley, New Jersey: creamy peanut butter and grape jelly on white bread—a good old, plain old, pb and j."

Mom, who knew my speech as well as I knew hers,

smiled absently and headed for her desk. Soon we'd both be heading for King Tut's Kitchen.

I went to my room to do my chemistry homework. But as soon as I flopped on the bed, I started thinking about the chemistry between the boy at the deli and me. We'd talked so easily, made each other laugh. If only Nora were here, we could talk about it.

I missed Nora a lot. We were almost exactly alike. She'd lived in my building, had gone to my school, and to the after-school photography class. The only difference was that she came from a traditional American family of mother, father, brother, sister, and dog. And they came from Japan. If Nora were here now, I'd tell her about the boy at the deli, and ask her what—if anything—to do about him.

I knew what Mom would say if I asked her what to do: "Your chemistry homework." Not that she'd ever stop me from going out with a boy. Just that she wanted me to be Ms. Prudent Student. So I ended up just going out in groups or to parties, never with any one boy.

Mrs. Nakamura was the same way. But at least Nora could talk to her mother about boys. I didn't feel comfortable doing that with Mom. I was kind of nervous about bringing up bad memories. Right after the divorce, Mom would start crying when we were just walking down the street. I was only eight, but I'd pat her arm and say, "It's okay, Mom." Sometimes she'd say, "Sweetheart, just go to your room and read for a while. I'll be fine." Then I knew she'd be *really* crying.

In my room I'd worry about her. After a while I'd start worrying that if I stayed in my room much longer, when I came out she'd be gone—like Dad. So I'd come out and massage her back to relax her or tell a joke to distract her. That crying time lasted only a few weeks, but boy, was I glad when she snapped out of it.

Soon after, Dad got a job offer in Denver, and moved. I saw him only during summer vacation. He married Wendy the next year. That's when Mom and I moved to New York. After that, Mom went out now and then, but didn't talk about her dates. Once I asked her about a guy. "Is he nice?" She smiled and said, "If he weren't, would I go out with him?" A couple of years later I asked about another. "What's he like?" She answered, "Nice."

Then last year Mom went out for months with Jack Crawford, another editor at her office. I liked him, and the three of us did stuff together. Around New Year's, they broke up, though. Mom told me at a Chinese restaurant. All she said was, "It didn't work out." The only way I knew she was trying not to cry was that she started studying the menu as if she were going to be tested on it. Then she switched the focus to me. "How about the cold noodles with sesame sauce to start with? Sesame sauce tastes something like peanut butter."

I could only guess how Mom felt, but I knew how I felt. I didn't want to start anything, and I didn't want anything exotic or anything that tasted like something else. A pb&j was what I wanted. Something simple, normal, and understandable. Something that wouldn't change.

Now I thought again about the boy at the deli—how he looked, what he said. I didn't know his first name and couldn't pronounce his last, but I couldn't stop thinking about him.

I moved to my desk and started my homework. A few minutes later, as I balanced a tricky equation, I remembered something Mom told me about how I first learned to talk. I was a little late putting words into sentences, she told me, but my first sentence was something terrific, like "I'm terribly sorry to have kept you waiting." Mom had said, "That sentence was worth waiting for." I looked up from my chemistry book and grinned. Maybe it would be the same with my first boyfriend.

All of a sudden, I did want to start something.

# 2

Tweed was waiting outside my building when I started for school Monday morning. His name was really Reed Thorpe the Fourth, but since most kids at our school dressed in shirts, jeans, and sneakers, and he showed up every day in a tweed suit, everybody called him Tweed Thorpe the Fourth.

Nobody could figure out why Tweed went to our school. He not only looked as if he went to Oxford University, he kind of acted it too. Once he came up to some kids who were talking about the basketball player Dr. J. and said, "Ah, yes, Dr. Johnson, the English wit immortalized by his biographer Boswell." Kids called him a show-off and a snob. I didn't really mind him, though. He made me laugh. I'd certainly never met anybody like him in Nutley, New Jersey.

"Do you want to be another Diane Arbus?" Tweed

asked, looking at my camera as he walked with me. Before I could open my mouth, he said, "Diane Arbus was a photographer who sort of specialized in the grotesque."

"I saw a book about her," I said. "She took some really weird pictures."

"You mean, she took pictures of really weird people," Tweed said. "Freaks."

"You think so? Don't you think maybe she made some of them *seem* freakish? I think she focused on the goofy parts of people, when she could've focused on other parts." I smiled at Tweed. "Anyway, I'm not another anybody."

Pushing his baby-fine brown hair from his blue eyes, Tweed seemed to give this some thought. "I didn't know you lived here in Yorkville," I said. Yorkville is a neighborhood famous for its old German butcher shops with window displays of pigs' heads. It's located in an elegant section of Manhattan called the Upper East Side.

"I don't live this far east," Tweed said.

"Where do you live?"

He cleared his throat. "Park Avenue."

Only rich people lived on Park Avenue. But so what? I grinned at him. "That's not around here? It's just four blocks west. You didn't need a passport to get over here, did you?"

Smiling slightly, he said, "Alexandra, are you teasing me?"

"Uh-huh," I said. "You ask for it." I glanced at my camera. "Speaking of passports, want me to take a new passport picture of you? Or how about a family portrait?"

Tweed's nose rose. "My passport's in order, and Mother's about to have the whole family done in oils."

"Olive or polyunsaturated corn?"

Tweed couldn't help laughing a little. Then he said, "The reason I'm here is, I want to immortalize you."

"What?"

"I want to write about you in my social studies paper on the American family. I want to be your Boswell, to write the story of your life."

"Me? *My* life? How come?"

"Because it's typical of our times," he said seriously.

"Tweed, I don't know what you're talking about. And even if I did, I'd feel weird telling anybody my life story. And even if I didn't, I'm only fifteen—what's to tell?"

"There's a lot to tell, no need to be embarrassed, and I'll explain what I'm talking about. Just meet me after school today, won't you?"

I didn't want to hurt anybody's feelings, but I also didn't want to tell anybody the story of my life. "Sorry, but I don't have time to be immortalized."

"I see," Tweed said, with almost an English accent. "You have no free time at all." Clearly he didn't believe me.

"I don't. I have"—what was a foolproof excuse he couldn't take personally?—"I have a job."

"A job?" Tweed looked as if he'd never heard the word before.

The school bell started ringing, and Tweed and I joined the other kids moving toward the school steps. But I kept thinking about a job. With a part-time job I could earn money for photography equipment. I wouldn't have to ask for a loan from Dad, who's a college professor and has as little money as Mom. I wouldn't have to wait to use the school darkroom, which was often occupied by kids making out. I had to work close to home

—Mom said no bus or subway alone after dark. So what neighborhood business could use help in the late afternoon and early evening?

The corner deli! Then I'd be near that boy maybe ten hours a week—520 hours a year, minimum. There was no Help Wanted sign in the window, but the place was packed from five to seven every weekday. I'd just walk in today and tell the boy's father they needed help.

Mom did something like that at work—she told bosses they needed to promote her. I helped her practice. Before she went for every promotion, we did something called role playing, which she read about in a book on how to get ahead. I played the role of Mom's boss and Mom played herself. By the time of her latest promotion, I was an old hand at role playing. I hammed it up, put my feet on her desk, chomped on her pen as if it were a cigar, and talked in a deep, gruff voice. "You think you can do the job, eh?" Mom looked me in the eye and said, "I *know* I can do it." I narrowed my eyes, blew smoke in her face. She didn't flinch. "Okay, you've got the job," I said. As we shook hands, Mom said, "You won't be sorry, Diana." I spit out my cigar. I'd forgotten that Mom's boss was a soft-spoken, nonsmoking woman.

I didn't go to the deli right after school. While the dismissal bell was still ringing, I was in the school darkroom. An hour later I was looking, all excited, at the roll of negatives. I couldn't wait to see the shots of the deli, and also the shots of the boy, which were sure to be—uh-oh. The first shot of the deli was a blur. The first shot of the boy was worse—a salami hanging inside the deli seemed to be growing out of his head. Quite a difference between my dreams of art and what I could actually do.

But wait . . . here was something. In one negative I

got the contrast between the old inside of the deli and the new outside surrounding it. And in another I got the boy, looking cute and nice. Fifteen minutes later I watched him appear on the print. I'd captured him. No matter where either of us went, I'd still have him with me as long as I had this picture.

Suddenly I remembered the first picture I ever took—a picture of Mom and Dad, when I was around seven. It was taken after one of their arguments, which ended as usual with Dad's going to his study. Mom took me outside to rake the autumn leaves, and I jumped in the leaf pile. When she got her camera to take my picture, I saw Dad looking through the kitchen window at us. "Daddy, come out!" I yelled. He came out, and I felt great. I asked if I could also take a picture. Mom showed me how. "I want to take a picture of Mommy and Daddy together," I said. They stood stiffly side by side. "Now hug," I said. They cracked up—and then they hugged. So much for *that* argument. I still had that picture. Anytime I wanted, I could see Mom and Dad together, laughing and hugging.

Somebody pounded on the door. "This darkroom belongs to the school, it's not your personal property," a kid called. "Come on out. I want a chance."

I got my stuff together, walked out the door, and out of school. I marched directly to the corner deli, where the owner was alone. After introducing myself, I reminded him how crowded his place was from five to seven on weekdays.

"I think you need another cashier," I said. "Me." Silence. I started to wilt. Then, drawing myself up, I looked him in the eye. "I mean, I *know* you need another cashier —me."

"You do, huh?" he growled.

Remembering how he yelled at his son, I was about to babble "But . . . uh . . . maybe not . . ."

"Okay, you got the job," he said.

"Pardon me?"

"You start tomorrow."

# 3

"Alexandra, do you think I'm sending you to private school so you can spend your evenings slicing salami?"

Mom wasn't home yet. I was sitting at her desk, pretending to be her.

I ran over to the sofa, folded my hands on my knees, and practiced my answer: "I won't be slicing salami, I'll be working the cash register. I'll be . . . uh . . . learning . . . growing . . . broadening my horizons."

Back to Mom's desk. I pretended to slash an *x* through an imaginary manuscript page, then asked, "What, exactly, will you be learning?"

The sofa again. After catching my breath, I held it until I thought of an answer: "Small-business administration."

I played Mom's role pretty well. That night she said everything I'd anticipated, right up to the final argument: "Alexandra, it'll be too much—school, photography, work, homework."

Looking her in the eye, I said, "Mom, if there's one thing you've taught me, it's the value of work. How many times have you told me how important it is?"

She stared at me, laughed, and pointed her pencil at me. "If even one of your grades goes down, that's the end of the job. Get it?"

Even though I hadn't rehearsed it, I ran across the room and threw my arms around her. "Got it!"

"You get it?" asked the deli owner the next day, after showing me how to operate the cash register.

"No problem," I said. I figured the hardest part was pronouncing his name right: Da-mas-ki-*na*-kis, I said to myself after he introduced himself: Damaskinakis, Damaskinakis, Damaskinakis.

"You go behind the other register, near my son. He'll make sure you do it right," Mr. Damaskinakis said.

From behind the other register, I smiled at the boy. "Hey, the famous filmmaker," he said. "I'm Heracles."

"Hercules? Like the strong man?"

"Close. Hercules was his Roman name. Heracles was his real name. He was a Greek hero. What's your name?"

"Alexandra Suss—"

"Gimme a roast beef on rye," interrupted a tall, broad-chested, middle-aged man wearing a lumber jacket and jeans.

"Sure. Just a second, please," Heracles said, turning back to me.

"And gimme some tomato," the man said. "And gimme some mayo . . . and gimme . . ."

"Give me a break," Heracles said, under his breath.

"Huh? My stomach's rumbling while you make time

with your girl, and I should give *you* a break?" the man said.

Red-faced, Heracles moved to the meat slicer and began cutting the beef. My face felt warm too.

"Have a heart, my dear fellow," said an old woman in a fur coat to the man. "You're only young once." I nodded agreement.

"The kid's got his whole life to make out with his girl," a young woman called over from the other checkout counter. "This poor clown's probably got twenty minutes for a lousy sandwich before his crummy night job." The man turned toward her. "Am I right?" she said.

"Right!" he said. Then his forehead creased as he seemed to think over that description. "Wait a minute . . ."

Some customers laughed, others joined the debate. Mr. Damaskinakis's voice boomed out in Greek. Even though I didn't understand the language, I got the message, and so did everybody else. We all shut up.

Heracles put the wrapped sandwich in a bag, and the bag on the counter, next to me.

"Hurry up, girlie," the man said.

I immediately assumed the role of the crisp, efficient cashier, quickly consulting the price list on the wall and smartly tapping out numbers on the register, even remembering to include the sales tax. The total came out $3,789.

"Three thousand seven hundred and eighty-nine bucks for a roast beef and tomato on rye?" the man bellowed. "Hey, I've only got two thousand on me. Hold the tomato."

The other customers roared with laughter. My face felt so hot, it almost hurt. I didn't even look at Heracles or

Mr. Damaskinakis. For the rest of the two hours, the place was so busy, and I was so determined not to mess up, that I hardly looked up from the cash register. When I said good night, Heracles smiled and saluted me with a chicken drumstick, but his father just nodded brusquely.

I trudged home. I'd thought it would be easy! As I wearily let myself into the apartment, the phone began ringing. I ran for it, tripped, fell. I answered the phone from the floor, taking off my shoes and rubbing my aching feet.

"Alexandra, I'm sorry. I was held up and I'm just leaving now," Mom said. "How was your first day at work?"

I closed my eyes and took a deep breath. "I learned . . . I grew . . . I broadened my horizons."

The rest of the week was rough. I yawned in school, the darkroom, and the deli. At night I fell asleep at my desk. The worst part was that Heracles and I hardly had time to talk. I found myself looking at him a lot, however. I didn't usually go all ga-ga about a boy's looks, but now I noticed how soft Heracles's hair seemed, how long his legs were, how his eyes kind of tilted up at the corners, and their color changed from dark brown to gold-brown. Near quitting time on Friday I looked at Heracles—and he was looking at me. It was the high point of my week.

That night, Mom and I had dinner at a Mexican restaurant, and between the guacamole and the enchiladas, I almost fell asleep. "Are you sure this job is working out for you?" Mom asked.

"Sure," I lied. The next day my lie turned into the truth.

# 4

When I picked up my paycheck on Saturday, I kissed it. I saw Heracles looking at me. We laughed. Seeing that his T-shirt was imprinted Just Visiting This Planet, I laughed again. "Nice shirt."

"Thanks." He nodded toward my check. "So, you spending or saving?"

"Both," I said. "Saving some for big photography equipment, spending some on film and filters so I can take pictures this morning. This afternoon I'm going to a new photography exhibit at the Metropolitan Museum."

"Sounds like a great day."

And he was stuck in his father's store all day. What a bummer. "Heracles!" his father called. As I left, Mr. Damaskinakis gave me kind of a dirty look. Was he mad at me for distracting Heracles? He seemed mad at Heracles all the time.

I shot a couple of rolls of film around the neighborhood, then went to the Metropolitan. As soon as I walked into the exhibit, I saw Heracles, looking at a picture.

I ran over to him. "I didn't know you were interested in photography."

"Me neither. I mean, I don't know anything about it. But after you mentioned the exhibit, I decided to come over on my lunch break and check it out."

"Want to check it out together?" I asked.

We had so much fun. After we looked at all the pictures, I asked Heracles which was his favorite. I figured he'd pick something funny. At first I thought he was kidding when he picked one called *Migrant Mother*. Taken during the Great Depression, it showed a young woman with pretty features but a sad expression holding onto her baby while two other little kids clung to her. When I asked Heracles why he liked it so much, he shrugged and said, "There's just something about it. . . . Which do you like best?"

My favorite showed three black kids playing tag in a vacant lot. For a minute I also had a hard time figuring out the reason for my choice. "Some people like pictures of great people or things or events—celebrities, the Grand Canyon, World War Two. But I like pictures of ordinary people doing ordinary things." I had to think some more. "What I especially like about this picture is that the photographer's caught an instant when the kids are just goofing around, but they're really really happy. So even though the picture shows ordinary life, it's beautiful, exciting, intense, and . . ." My face began to burn. "I never talked about pictures before. Do I sound weird? I sound weird, don't I?"

"Nope," Heracles said. "Trust me, I'm an expert on weirdness."

I laughed. "Really?"

"I bought myself this T-shirt because it tells what my family thinks of me. They think I'm from outer space, and they don't even know what I'm really like."

"They don't?" I asked, wanting him to go on.

Heracles shook his head, but didn't say any more. We walked out of the museum together. The cold air felt great. "See any pictures now?" Heracles asked.

I looked out at the wide steps, the people, Fifth Avenue. Slipping my camera strap over my head, I focused on the pretzel vendor handing an enormous pretzel to an elegant old man. Shoonck. A little girl chasing a helium-filled balloon. Shoonck. When I looked at Heracles, he was looking at me. We smiled at each other, and I thought, Right now, I'm really really happy. I wish I had a picture of this instant.

Looking at his watch, Heracles said, "Hey, I gotta go." He seemed about to say something else, then just waved and took those long strides away. As soon as he left my side, I missed him.

When he got across the street, he turned and ran back. "Listen, tomorrow on my lunch break I'm going to the Museum of Natural History's new exhibit. Want to go? It's about simians. Personally, I go ape over them."

"Seriously?" I said. "Don't monkey around with me." We left each other laughing. As I walked home, I imagined my heart beating in a new rhythm: *Her*-a-cles *Her*-a-cles *Her*-a-cles. I laughed it off.

Sometimes on Sundays Mom and I hung out together. This Sunday I planned to tell her I had to go to the museum to research a school science project. I could say

I was meeting Heracles, but I didn't want her to ask questions or worry or make a big deal.

Before I could say anything, though, Mom spoke up. She was surrounded by sections of the Sunday *New York Times* and was munching on a bagel with cream cheese and lox. Even though Mom was raised a Catholic, she liked Jewish food as much as my father, who *was* Jewish, did. "Sweetheart, would you mind very much if I did some work here at home today," she said, "instead of doing something with you?"

I gulped down my bite of bagel with peanut butter and jelly. "I don't mind at all."

I was at the museum when Heracles arrived. As soon as I saw him, my heart started beating faster. Checking out the apes together, we had as much fun as the day before. I even laughed at Heracles's imitation of King Kong, and he even laughed at my pun that it was "chimply terrific."

Afterwards I said, "I've seen some incredible pictures of chimps. A woman anthropologist lived in the African wild, studied the chimps, and wrote a book about it. A guy with her took the pictures."

"Want to be a team?" Heracles said. "I could study the apes, you could take their pictures." My heart started beating double-time. Smiling, Heracles said, "Come see my favorite exhibit." A few minutes later we were sitting on the steps in the Ocean Mammal Room, staring at the hundred-foot-long blue whale.

"Wow," I said.

"I come to the museum sometimes just to look at the whale," Heracles said. "It makes me feel calm."

I turned toward him. His eyes were gold now. His skin seemed lighter than usual, his hair even darker. "You're not calm all the time?"

He kept looking straight ahead. "Yeah, well, some people keep their—what's that word?—their chaos inside them."

Before I could say anything, he stood up. He helped me up, and we began walking through the museum. "So you're interested in science," I said.

"Science, science fiction, sci-fi and horror movies. Even science puns. Got any more?"

"Sure. Mr. Horowitz, my chemistry teacher, started it by saying, 'Old chemists never die, they just fail to react.' The kids started saying stuff like 'Friction, what a drag' and 'Gravity gets me down.' "

Heracles laughed. "What's your favorite science fiction or horror movie?"

"Somehow I've never seen any," I said.

"You don't know what you're missing. You've got to see at least one."

Would he ask me to see one with him? I waited . . . and waited . . . "I hope your school has a good science program," I said.

"I go to the Bronx High School of Science."

"I'm impressed. It's one of the best schools in New York, public or private. I know it's really hard to get into."

He put his hands in his pockets. "Getting into college'll be a lot harder. I want to get my B.S., M.S., and Ph.D. from Stanford, which has the best genetics program in the country, and even has a patent on the kind of research I want to do."

"Stanford's in California, right?"

"Yeah. Expensive too. Papa doesn't want me to go out of the store, much less across the country. I'd need full scholarships all the way."

I wanted to say I'd give him the money. As if I had it! For the first time I thought how lucky I was that Mom encouraged me to think about the best schools, regardless of cost.

Heracles was looking at his watch. "Uh-oh. Gotta go."

I blurted, "Heracles, if you want to, you can let *me* know what you're really like."

Silence. I'd faint if he just walked away, or laughed, or said "Huh?"

"I want to," he said softly.

The wind blew my hair across my face. Heracles pushed it back very, very gently. "You have pretty hair," he said.

"So do you," I said.

We laughed, then suddenly stopped, and I saw Heracles gulp. "See you tomorrow," he said. I watched him as he got smaller and smaller and finally disappeared. Even then I kept looking.

# 5

Heracles was the last thing I thought of before I went to sleep that night and the first thing I thought of when I woke up the next morning. I also thought of him during the day. In chemistry class I was daydreaming about him when I was supposed to be thinking about covalent bonds. "Earth to Alexandra, Earth to Alexandra," Mr. Horowitz called, making everybody laugh, even me. Everything was nicer because of Heracles—jokes were funnier, the sun was sunnier, I was happier.

Before I reported to the deli that day, I peeked in the window. Heracles goofed around by looking at me through a hole in a slice of Swiss cheese. I was laughing, when suddenly I was pushed from behind so hard, I was knocked against the window. "Ow!" My forehead hit the glass. Holding my head, I saw a skinny, wild-haired kid around nine or ten years old running into the store, and I ran after him.

He ran up to Mr. Damaskinakis. Ha! Now he'd get what he deserved from old Mr. Mean. But Mr. Damaskinakis's face lit up. "Theo!" He kissed the kid on one cheek, then the other, and hugged him tight, murmuring, "My baby." The kid had to be Heracles's little brother! As Mr. Damaskinakis took him by the hand toward the back of the store, a customer asked me a question, and I went to work.

It turned out I'd improved at the job since the week before, so Heracles and I had much more time to talk. For the rest of the week we talked about science and art, books and pictures and movies, public school and private school, New Jersey and New York.

I liked Heracles more every day. He was as dark as I was fair—like the negative and print of a picture—but we both liked to listen as well as to talk, and we both joked and laughed a lot. We had such a terrific time together that every day when I went to work I expected him to ask me out. He didn't though.

On Friday, when I was just about to leave, there were no customers at my register or his counter, and Mr. Damaskinakis was busy counting money. Now was the time. Say it, I told myself, say it. "Heracles, *Dr. Jekyll and Mr. Hyde* is playing at the Regency on Sunday. Want to go with me?" Heracles hesitated. Was it too late for me to take it back? Then he smiled. "Sure."

On Saturday Mom said it was okay for me to make a twenty-minute phone call to Nora. Mom was out when I made the call, which lasted an hour and fifteen minutes. What could I do? It took me ten minutes just to tell Nora about his hair. I'd only worked my way down to his shoulders when she interrupted to tell me about *two* boys she had crushes on.

Later I asked Mom if I could get some new clothes, knowing she'd be surprised but say yes. I hardly ever bought new clothes; the older the better was usually my motto. Since I was tall and thin like Mom, I'd not only inherited her genes, I could inherit her jeans. I never let her throw any out. Today, though, I went to six stores, trying on nine pairs of jeans and ten tops. What color sweater would Heracles like? Blue? Black? Red? What about a T-shirt, like he wore? There was even a *Star Trek* special: Beam Me Up, Scotty, There's No Intelligent Life Down Here. But did I want him to laugh at my chest? I ended up with baggy blue jeans and a cranberry sweater, and even new socks—blue, black, and cranberry stripes.

I took a bath and washed my hair Saturday night. Sunday morning I woke at dawn. What was Heracles doing that minute? I wondered. Could he be thinking of me? Then I realized that he was probably sleeping, like a normal person. I sure wasn't normal anymore. Or was I normal now for the first time? Leaping out of bed at six A.M., I made myself a pb&j. As the spongy softness of the bread, the sweet gloppiness of the jelly, and the smooth nuttiness of the peanut butter mingled in my mouth, something finally came together in my head. Postponing my bath, I sat down at my desk to write a letter. "Dear Nora," I wrote. "I'm in love."

I met Heracles at the bus stop on Sunday afternoon. "So this is your first," he said.

Oh, my God. Was it that obvious that this was my first date with my first love?

"Your first monster movie," he said with a smile.

What a relief. "Should I practice saying 'Eeek!'?"

"Not necessarily," Heracles said. "A science fiction writer once gave a speech that started, 'I love monsters.'

He went on to say what an interesting guy Mr. Hyde was, compared to that cowardly nerd Dr. Jekyll."

I laughed. "Who are your favorite monsters?"

"In books, Mr. Hyde. In movies, the phantom of the opera. In real life, Papa."

Just then the crosstown bus pulled up. During the ride we talked about movies, then at Broadway we got off the bus and walked toward the theater.

"Forget I said that about Papa," Heracles said. "He came to this country by himself when he was just eleven years old, without anything. He couldn't even speak the language. In ten years he'd bought this store and was supporting relatives in Greece." Shaking his head, Heracles said, "Papa's an amazing man. I admire him. Sometimes I wish . . . I wish I didn't."

I wanted to know more, but we were in front of the theater, and Heracles stopped talking. Inside, it was wonderful to sit so close to him that we were almost touching. Because he'd told me about his father, I felt close to him in another way. For the next two hours I felt as if I were in a dream. *Dr. Jekyll and Mr. Hyde* wasn't really scary. It was an excellent movie though.

"So, are you a monster lover too?" Heracles asked, as we left the theater.

"Uh-huh."

He held out his hand. "Welcome to the club." When we shook, I noticed that his eyes were dark today, and his eyelashes long, his cheekbones high, his mouth . . . well, sensual was probably the word. He was looking at me too. It was a long time before we let go of each other's hands.

Walking to the bus stop, I asked, "Do you think everybody's like Dr. Jekyll? We all have a monster inside?"

"Yeah. But I agree with that science fiction writer. Sometimes, in a way, the monster's not the worst part of people; it's the best. I mean, it's not just anger or aggression, or negative things. It's . . . I'm not sure how to say it."

"You mean, sometimes people kind of lock up their energy and creativity? They keep it hiding inside?"

Stopping and smiling, he said, "I'm always telling you stuff I never told anybody, Alexandra, and you really understand." I thought my smile would never stop.

After we sat down in the back of the bus, Heracles said, "Hey, remember *Attack of the Giant Killer Sandwich?*"

"I'll never forget it," I said. "But maybe the movie should be set in a fancy gourmet deli—*Attack of the Giant Killer Quiche.*"

"No way. It's in a *Greek* deli. It should be *Attack of the Giant Killer Feta Cheese.*"

"It could get hot and slimy and ooze all over the store," I said, laughing.

"People could get stuck in the gook." Heracles was also laughing.

"Glub glub glub," we said at exactly the same time, then laughed so loud that people turned around to look at us.

Getting off the bus, we were laughing so hard, he was holding his stomach and I was making these weird breathless hoots. "Hoot! Hoot!" Every time one of us stopped laughing, the other started again.

Wiping his eyes, Heracles said, "Want to walk over to the river to calm down?"

I didn't care where we went, I just didn't want this day to end. On the walkway, looking at the river, we did calm down. In back of us stood high-rise apartments where thousands of people lived, below us were highways where streams of cars sped north and south. But Heracles and I were alone together.

"Here's something else I never told anybody," Heracles said, his voice soft and serious. "I remember a movie —or maybe it was a dream—where a guy was getting on the downtown subway, and he looked across at the other platform and saw a girl getting on the uptown subway. I knew the guy was thinking, I wish I could know that girl, maybe that girl could change my whole life."

Watching the river, I said, "Maybe the girl was thinking the same thing."

We looked at each other, and the river breeze that pushed my hair back, pushed his forward. I wanted to touch those dark curls. I did. Then, almost in slow motion, we leaned toward each other and kissed. My first kiss. My first love.

Heracles said, "Alexandra, what I've been trying to tell you is, I already have a girlfriend."

# 6

"Oh." My voice came out high as a little kid's. "Sure. I knew that," I lied. My smile felt like a sword slashing my face as I said, "Well, gotta go."

I walked very quickly and Heracles kept up, but we didn't talk to each other. Not out loud, anyway. Silently, I was asking myself the questions I wanted to ask him.

Question: Why didn't you tell me? Answer: You didn't ask. Question: Why did you act like you liked me? Answer: I do like you. I like a lot of people. I even like monsters. Question: Why did you get together with me at the photography exhibit, the simian exhibit, and the movie? Answer: I like pictures, I like apes, and I already told you I like monsters. I paused before I asked the next question, even to myself: And the kiss? Why did you kiss me? Slowing down for a second, I came up with an answer: Why not?

" 'Night," I called, my back to Heracles, as we approached my building. "Alexandra?" When he called, I was already opening the door. "Alexandra!"

Coming home to the empty apartment, I felt my face kind of crumple. I didn't want Mom to see me upset, but I suddenly did want to see Mom. I sort of missed her. It looked like she was right and I was better off being Ms. Prudent Student than really getting involved with a boy. I should start my homework, so I'd keep getting good grades, go to a top college, get a B.A. and an M.B.A. Never mind the B.O.Y. I wouldn't date until I was vice-president of a major corporation . . . or the country. I walked into my room, still persuading myself to start studying. Then I saw my latest prints, thumb-tacked to the bulletin board: The little girl chasing the balloon . . . Heracles outside the deli . . .

My eyes filled with tears, but I blinked them back. After that crying time of Mom's, I didn't want to see any more tears, not even my own. Also, I had allergies. When I cried, somehow it wasn't just my eyes that got the workout, it was my nose. Blowing my nose, I decided to quit my job at the deli. No way I'd hang around Heracles ten hours a day, 520 hours a year. Well . . . at least I'd learned a little about small-business administration.

And I'd learned and grown by asking Heracles out and even by kissing him, right? I'd broadened my horizons. How did that poem go—it is better to have loved and lost than . . . than what? It is better to have loved and lost than to have loved and won? That couldn't be right. It was better to have loved and lost . . . than never to have loved at all. So there!

Maybe with the money I earned in the last two weeks I could start buying some used photography equipment.

Maybe I could even earn money for more equipment by taking portraits and developing them in the school darkroom! I'd make an ad tonight, and put it on the school bulletin board tomorrow. I blew my nose again, loud as a trumpet. I'd be fine, just fine. I'd be normal and happy in no time at all.

The next day I arrived at the deli feeling pretty good, considering. I planned to act normal. I was definitely prepared to see Heracles. Too bad I wasn't prepared to see his girlfriend.

As soon as I stepped inside, she came into view. Right away I remembered the day the Pizzutello twins, Lori and Gloria, came into our sixth-grade classroom, bringing with them the first fully developed breast . . . and also the second, third, and fourth. Who could compete? Heracles's girlfriend was petite, very curvy, and cute, with hair as dark as his and eyes even darker. Dressed in tight jeans and a tight, fuzzy sweater, she snuggled against him. Mr. Damaskinakis beamed. I tried not to throw up.

"Alexandra . . ." Heracles began.

"Hi, I'm Eleni," the girl interrupted in a deep, womanly voice with a strong New York accent. "I'm Heracles's girlfriend."

How subtle! Did she have a sweatshirt with this identification?

"We've been going together for a long time," she said.

Maybe she had a few old corsages she'd care to show me? A commemorative hickey or two she'd like to point out?

"Four years," she said, gazing up at Heracles as if he were a god. Girlfriend? This was a catty, competitive girl*fiend*. She could star in her own horror movie.

"*My* boyfriend and *I* have been going together for *five* years," I heard someone say. Me! I was the one who said it! In my whole life, I'd never told a crazy lie like that. Five years ago I was ten years old. My only hope was that Eleni couldn't subtract.

"Yeah? What's your boyfriend's name?" she asked.

"Oh, God," I blurted. Who'd ever expect her to ask that?

"What?"

"Osgood," I said. "Osgood Podhurst the Third."

Eleni giggled. "That's a funny name." This from the girlfriend of Heracles Damaskinakis! "Why don't you bring Osgood around? We could double-date," she said. Heracles bit his lip.

"What a shame," I said coolly, "that he's away at . . . at Yale . . . studying . . . mmm . . . ah . . . medieval literature." Uh-oh. *Was* there any medieval literature? Or only minstrels, singing stuff like "hey nonny nonny" instead of writing stories down? I hoped Heracles was as ignorant about this as I was. No problem with Eleni.

"Heracles is smart too," Eleni said. "But he doesn't want to go away to college. He wants to stay right here and help Papa Damaskinakis in the store."

He did? What was she talking about? I looked at Heracles, who was staring in the meat case at the baloney. Well, whatever she was talking about, it was none of my business. "Heracles, I'm giving your father notice now," I said. I waved at Eleni. Then I walked over to Mr. Damaskinakis, thanked him for the chance to learn and earn, and quit.

"You don't have to give no notice," he said. "Eleni, she'll always help me out." He winked at Eleni, who

giggled in reply. Heracles started slicing meat. So . . .
Heracles's father and girlfriend were united in wanting
him to work in the store for the rest of his life. It was a
shame. Personally, I wasn't going to hang around here
for one more minute.

# 7

Outside, a cold wind hit me. Putting my head down, I pushed forward. How weird, Heracles's not telling his father and girlfriend that he wanted to go to Stanford. What was he waiting for? When his hair was as white as his father's, would he still be waiting?

As I opened the door to my building, I thought, Somebody should help Heracles stand up for himself. He should *assert* himself—that was the word. Last year Mom took a lunchtime course at the Y to learn how to assert herself better at work, and she told me a little about it. Unlocking the apartment door, I thought, maybe *I* should help Heracles assert himself. Maybe I should get together with him for human rights, instead of romance.

Then in my room I looked at his picture, sighed, and almost cried. My stomach felt queasy as I remembered saying I had a boyfriend. I'd better forget about Heracles. A normal, happy person didn't go around sighing, crying, feeling sick to her stomach, and lying. Okay, it was better to have loved and lost than never to have loved at all. But now it was better to keep Heracles out of my life and get busy with other things.

I got busy all week with other things. I took lots of pictures. I made chicken pilaf, Mom's favorite dinner. I hung out after school with Dana Trehuba and Brooke McNichol, girls from my homeroom. I worked so hard on my history report that the teacher, Mr. Iasevoli, gave me his special reward—instead of "brownie points" for outstanding work, he handed out real brownies he'd baked himself.

I still missed Heracles though—more every day. Finally, on Saturday afternoon when I was on my way to take pictures, I peeked in the deli window. Mr. Damaskinakis was there, Eleni wasn't. As soon as I saw Heracles, he saw me. Right away, he started juggling apples and oranges. He kept dropping them, but he also kept smiling. Who could help smiling back a little? Heracles came out.

"Hey, Alexandra, how've you been? Taking lots of pictures?" His voice cracked on the last word.

"Sure." I meant to pat my camera confidently, but I ended up smacking it hard, hurting my hand. I tried not to show it though. "I put an ad on the school bulletin board. I want to make some money by doing portraits."

"Have I got a job for you!" Heracles said.

"You want me to take your portrait? For your girlfriend?" I couldn't help sounding a little hurt.

"My brother Theo's. To give to Papa for his birthday."

"Oh." Yuch, the bratty little brother. But it was really

for Heracles. "Fine, except you don't have to pay." Save your money for Stanford, I wanted to say.

"Don't be nuts. Of course, I'll pay," Heracles said. "Tomorrow afternoon in our apartment? We live right over the store."

"Okay." I suddenly realized that I'd never seen Heracles's mother. "Heracles, are your parents divorced?"

He looked surprised. "My mother died of cancer when I was ten."

This was such a surprise to me, I felt as if I'd been punched in the stomach. "Oh, I'm so sorry."

"Don't worry about it. I hardly remember her," Heracles said.

"Really? I remember things that happened to me when I was tiny. I remember toddling around the public library, pulling picture books off the bottom shelf for Mom to read to me." How dopey of me to go on about my mother. I searched for something else to say. "So, did your father get a replacement for me in the deli?"

Heracles looked at the sidewalk before he looked at me. "Eleni." He cleared his throat. "And how's Osgood?"

My voice came out an octave higher than usual. "Same as ever."

"He's studying literature, right? He must have interesting things to say. At least he can quote stuff. What can a scientist say—E equals MC squared?"

I laughed.

"Wait a minute—I could quote from a monster movie," Heracles said. Flinging an imaginary cape over his shoulder, he said, "Velcome to my lab-*or*-at'ry."

"You're really silly," I said, laughing again.

"Face it, Alexandra. You bring out the beast in me."

We just looked at each other for a few seconds. I wouldn't let myself love him, but I couldn't help liking him. I really couldn't.

"Hey, I've missed you," he said.

"I've missed you too."

"Heracles!" That was Mr. Damaskinakis's voice, from inside the store. "Alexandra!" Another, lighter voice came from across the street, and Heracles and I turned toward it.

"That's Osgood, right?" Heracles said. "You don't even have to tell me that's Osgood Podhurst the Third, home from Yale for the weekend." Without waiting for an answer, Heracles went back in the store.

# 8

"Hi, there, Alexandra," Tweed said, after he came across the street and stood next to me.

I wanted to tell Heracles that Tweed wasn't Osgood, but Heracles was already working, and Mr. Damaskinakis was scowling out the window at me. I walked toward the park, Tweed walking along.

"I'm here about your ad," Tweed said.

Wow, what a surprise. "You want me to take your portrait?"

"Not mine," he said. "Another Thorpe's."

"Whose?"

"Winnie's."

"Your sister?"

"My schnauzer."

The Metropolitan's photography exhibit flashed through my mind: Julia Margaret Cameron's portrait of

Darwin . . . Margaret Bourke-White's portrait of Gandhi . . . Alexandra Susskind's portrait of Winnie? "Uh, no thanks, Tweed."

His blue eyes widening, Tweed said, "But Winnie's full name is Winston Churchill Thorpe. He's related to dogs owned by British aristocracy. He has papers."

"I hope he knows how to use them. Otherwise his name could be Winnie the Poop."

"That's gross," Tweed said, but he laughed.

"I'll tell you what," I said. "I'll take your portrait. If you like it, buy it; if not, forget it. That's how confident I am."

"That's how desperate you are."

I laughed. "You're right. How about giving me a chance?" When Tweed hesitated, I said, "If you'll let me take your picture, I'll let you interview me for your paper."

He stared at me for a minute. "Oh, all right."

"All riiiiight!" I grinned. "Where and when?"

"This Sunday around six at my home. It's on the corner of Eighty-first and . . ."

"I know—Park Avenue. Good thing my passport's in order."

The next day I went to Damaskinakis's deli early, kind of hoping Heracles and I could talk before I took Theo's picture. As soon as I got inside, Mr. Damaskinakis started giving Heracles orders—pick this up, put that down.

The door swung open. "Wheeeeee!" In came Theo—on a skateboard. "Whoooooa!" He crashed into a counter, knocking over a glass jar filled with candies. Gumballs, lollipops, and jawbreakers scattered all over the floor.

Heracles, his father, and I bent to pick them up. Theo picked up one piece. "Hey, want a pop, Pop?"

Mr. Damaskinakis shook his head. Theo unwrapped the pop and stuck it in his own mouth. "Your teacher said no candy for you," Mr. Damaskinakis said mildly.

"No more after this, Pop." As soon as Mr. Damaskinakis turned his back, Theo picked up a handful of pops and stuffed them in his jeans pocket.

"Hey!" I said, looking at Heracles, who was also watching Theo, but Heracles just looked away.

"Anybody in the mood to wait on a customer?" an old woman called cheerfully from the cash register.

"Sure, sure. I'll be right there." Mr. Damaskinakis hustled over to the counter, followed by Theo, while Heracles and I finished picking up the candies. Patting Theo on the shoulder, Mr. Damaskinakis smiled at the customer. "You know my son Theo."

The woman smiled. "My goodness, you're getting to be a big boy, Theo. How old are you now?"

"I'm a thirty-year-old midget," Theo said.

"Theo!" Mr. Damaskinakis put his big hand on Theo's bony shoulder and whispered in his ear.

"Yeah yeah yeah," Theo mumbled.

"I apologize for my son," Mr. Damaskinakis said to the customer. Wrapping his arms around Theo, he said, "You're a good boy." I thought, If Theo's a good boy, I'm Princess Di. Just then Mr. Damaskinakis turned to me. "Go upstairs and get your camera ready, huh?"

The Damaskinakis family's apartment had a lot more furniture than Mom's and mine, and a lot less light. After a few minutes I tiptoed down the hall and looked in the bedroom. Heracles and Theo shared it, and there was no question which side of the room was whose. One side was neat and almost bare, with a Museum of Natural History poster thumb-tacked to the wall above the bed. On the other side clothes, toys, and comic books were scattered all over; crayoned right on the wall were incredibly elaborate drawings of airplanes dropping bombs, rockets going off, soldiers shooting machine guns.

Hearing footsteps on the stairs, I quickly tiptoed back into the living room.

"Outta my way, I gotta piss!" Theo shouted, slamming the door and racing down the hall to the bathroom.

Was this really the best way to start my career? Maybe I'd be better off with a schnauzer. I took a step toward the door.

There were more footsteps on the stairs, and Mr. Damaskinakis came in. "Hiya, Alexandra," he said, calling me by name for the first time. As his eyes searched for his son, Theo came thundering back into the room. "Hey, you," he said to me.

"My name's Alexandra."

"Pick a nose," he said. He pointed at the middle of my face, his father's face, and his own. "Come on, pick a nose. Which one?"

"I pick yours," I said.

"Now that you picked it, what're you gonna do with it?" Theo laughed so hard, he fell on the floor.

"Good joke, Theo," I said, smiling. "Now, how about sitting on the couch?"

After Mr. Damaskinakis helped him up, Theo sat for two seconds, then began bouncing.

"Sit still—okay?" I was no longer smiling.

"Theo's a nice boy," Mr. Damaskinakis said. Theo stopped bouncing. "See?" Mr. Damaskinakis said to me.

While he was looking at me, I looked at Theo—who put his thumbs in his ears and wiggled his fingers.

My voice louder than usual, I said, "I'm going to count, and when I get to three I want you to stay still for just one minute, Theo. One . . . two . . ."

"What'd you stop for?" Mr. Damaskinakis said. "Look how still he is."

He was still—but his eyes were crossed. I closed my eyes and counted to ten to stop myself from smashing my camera over Theo's head. I didn't want to hurt my camera.

"Maybe I'm making the boy nervous," Mr. Damaskinakis said. He kissed Theo on both cheeks and left.

I took a real deep breath. "Theo, your brother wants to give this picture of you to your father for a birthday present. So let's have the very best view of Theo Damaskinakis, okay?" I even smiled

I focused. Theo was still. I put my finger on the shutter release. He stayed still. As I pushed the release, he spun around, pulled down his pants, and mooned me.

# 9

"Pull up your pants, you little monster!" I shouted.

I heard fast footsteps on the stairs, and Mr. Damaskinakis rushed in, breathless. "What's the matter?"

When I turned to Theo his eyes were wide and his pants back where they belonged.

"Alexandra, what's wrong? My boy's all right, isn't he?"

"Theo was . . ." Mr. Damaskinakis looked so scared that I couldn't say it. "He was having a hard time sitting still."

"Maybe he's tired today," Mr. Damaskinakis said. "You'll come back when he's not so beat, huh?"

"Sure." I put on my coat, picked up my camera, and walked downstairs. Heracles was waiting on a customer, and I didn't interrupt him. I just walked out to the street. What a little brat Theo was! But Mr. Damaskinakis was sweet to him, and mean to Heracles. It was weird. And it wasn't right!

As usual, when I got upset, I got busy. At home, I started defrosting the refrigerator. Mom disliked housework. I kidded her that her schedule for cleaning the oven was never—when it got too cruddy, we moved. But I enjoyed making things in our home look good and work right.

Mom looked up from the Sunday *Times*. "Alexandra, you don't have to struggle with the ice like that. It'll soon melt or fall off by itself."

"I know, I know." I pulled off a big chunk of ice from the top of the freezer and threw it in the sink. Crash!

"When your father was upset, he used to sleep."

Mom was giving me an opening to tell her Yeah, I was upset—and why. I grappled with a piece of ice. Pull. Push. Wiggle. Aha! Crash! "I haven't heard from Dad in almost a week. He should be calling any day."

"Sweetheart, there's somebody *I* haven't heard from in a while," Mom said.

Crash! "Who?"

"You. We haven't had a good talk in weeks."

I kept working. What could I say? Where could I start? I didn't feel like getting into it.

"Alexandra, is there anything you want to tell me?"

"Yeah. This sink could use a scouring."

The phone rang, and I answered it. "Alexandra, it's Heracles. I have to talk to you. Tomorrow after school can we meet away from the deli?"

"Sure. Want to come to my school?" I gave him the address. After I hung up, I closed the freezer door and dried my hands in one second. "Hey, Mom, any good old movies on TV?"

It felt really strange to come out of school the next day and see Heracles there waiting for me. It also felt really nice.

"Hi." He looked around and whistled. "Some school."

"The building used to be a rich family's mansion. They donated it to the school. Want a tour?"

"Yeah, but first I want to tell you something." He sat on the school steps, and I sat next to him. Looking right at me, he said, "Theo has a problem, Alexandra. He's had it since he was born."

I opened my mouth, surprised that Theo wasn't just an obnoxious kid.

"Sometimes people think he's retarded or disturbed," Heracles said, still facing me. "But he's not, he's really not." His shoulders slumped a little, then he lifted them. "As far as what his problem really is, first the doctor said he was 'hyperactive.' Now the school says he has some kind of 'learning disability.' Five years ago when he started school the teachers called him 'hyperactive.' Now they say he has a 'minimal brain dysfunction' or an 'attention-deficit disorder.' "

"I'm sorry, Heracles." Boy, how many troubles could a family have? "Does Theo go to a special school?"

"A special class in public school. He's smart. It's just almost impossible for him to focus on any one thing though. Everything excites him. He gets out of control."

"Thanks for telling me," I said. "If I knew before, I wouldn't have gotten so mad at him when I was trying to take his picture. Your father didn't say anything to me about it."

"Yeah, right." Heracles nodded. "Papa doesn't say

anything to me about it either. That's one of our basic family rules—never talk about anything important."

Without thinking, I said, "Does that mean you and your father and brother don't talk about your mother?"

Heracles stood and looked across the street, where two kids around Theo's age were whispering and laughing. "How about that tour of your school?"

We walked inside. "Hey, high ceilings and a spiral staircase," he said. "Bronx Science sure doesn't look this good."

"But Nobel prize winners came from your school. It must be really inspiring." I knew then where I wanted to take Heracles. "Come see my favorite part of school."

As we walked, Heracles looked like his mind was far away. On his brother? His mother? What a rotten deal for his family. When we got to our destination, I tried to make him smile. "Velcome to my lab-*or*-at'ry," I said, opening the darkroom door.

Heracles laughed, then I walked into the darkness and he followed. As soon as we got inside, the door closed, and I realized that the light switch was next to him. I turned fast—and bumped the top of my head against the middle of his face.

"Oh, no." In the dark, I peered at his face. "Did I hurt you?"

Gingerly Heracles touched the space between the bottom of his nose and his upper lip. "I'll live," he said with a smile.

I smiled back. We kept smiling at each other. Then I babbled, "I just thought of the weirdest thing. My mother told me the name for that part of your face."

"The philtrum," Heracles said.

"I can't believe you know that!"

"It's a Greek word. Did your mother tell you what it meant?" When I shook my head, Heracles said, "It means . . ." His voice got much softer. "Well, the thing is, it means . . ." He cleared his throat. " 'Love potion.' "

A short silence, then my voice was even softer than his. "Oh? . . . Well, gee . . . maybe there's a lot my mother didn't tell me."

Another silence. I realized how dark and small this room was. Heracles and I were so close together that if either of us moved at all, we'd touch each other. We couldn't help it. If I didn't turn on the light right now, we could end up doing something crazy—like kissing.

"Come on, hurry up."

It took me a couple of seconds to realize that the words came from outside the darkroom door. A kid wanted to get in.

I turned on the light, Heracles and I looked at each other for just a second, then he looked at his watch.

Quickly I said, "I'd like another try at Theo's picture. Would it be good to get him away from the store? I could take him to the park, say, Saturday afternoon."

"It'd be great. But you'd better not do it alone. Since it's for Theo, Papa might let me off work for a while. Mind if I come too?"

I smiled. "I'll live."

Heracles put his hand on the doorknob and said, "I guess Osgood doesn't mind if you're friendly with other guys."

"What? Oh, no. Osgood's very . . . mature."

"He's a good-looking guy too," Heracles said. "And Yale's not real far away. I guess you see him a lot."

"Not so much," I said. "We're both so busy."

"But he probably writes to you and calls you all the time," Heracles said.

"And now that you and Eleni are working right alongside each other Monday through Friday, you two must be closer than ever," I said.

Heracles hesitated. "Alexandra, what I've talked to you about—Papa, Theo, Stanford—I never told anybody else." Before I could say anything, he was gone.

# 10

Shoonck. On my way home, I took pictures of the pots of tulips outside a florist's shop. Spring was coming! Soon tulips would be blooming in the middle of Park Avenue. Tulips were my favorite flower, spring my favorite season, and Heracles my favorite person. He was not only cute and smart and funny, he was really nice. I was so glad he was my friend. I couldn't wait for Saturday.

At home I got a call from the mother of Nell Donaldson, a girl in my English class. Mrs. Donaldson asked if I'd take a portrait of her younger kids. Before she finished the sentence, I said yes. Sunday afternoon? The sooner the better.

It looked like I'd be out of the house practically all weekend. I wasn't sure I wanted to tell Mom how much time and energy I was spending on my hobby instead of my homework, though. So I told her I was doing library research on Saturday and museum research on Sunday. She said meanwhile she'd be spending a little extra time at the office. I was surprised, since she'd never gone to the office on a weekend before, but I didn't have time to think about it. She and I made plans to go to the Regency Saturday night and see Cary Grant and Katharine Hepburn in *Bringing Up Baby,* a funny old movie.

I practically danced over to the deli on Saturday afternoon. Heracles was wearing a red hooded sweatshirt that looked great with his black hair. We greeted each other with giant smiles. Theo continued blowing a bubble that was already as big as his face. "Theo, say hi to Alexandra," Heracles said.

Pop! Theo peeled the gum from his face.

As Heracles and I started walking south, Theo ran west, crossing the street against the light. When he got to the sidewalk, I called out, "Theo, how about walking the way we're walking?"

"I never walk the way Heracles walks," he yelled back.

Trying to be clever, I said, "So how about walking the way *I'm* walking?"

"Ha ha. What do I look like—a fag?" Theo spun around and wiggled west.

Turning to Heracles, I asked, "What now?"

"I've got a terrific idea. We'll walk the way he's walking."

I told Heracles two new puns from my chemistry class. "Botanists get to the root of things," and "Entomologists bug you."

He said, "I've got one about geneticists—they peek in your genes." I hit him on the arm. We had a great time just walking and talking together all the way to the park.

Then Theo ran to the edge of the sailboat pond. He

leaned forward, turned his arms in circles, and yelled, "Help!" I dropped my camera and ran like mad to save him from falling in. As soon as I reached him, he straightened up, laughed, and thumbed his nose at me.

Boy, did I feel stupid. Mad too. Theo acted as if he wanted everybody to watch him and worry about him all the time. If he could do that, couldn't he behave himself? Then I felt ashamed—Theo was doing the best he could.

What a relief when he moved away from the water, and Heracles and I could sit looking at the serene and pretty pond. "Once my friend Nora Nakamura and I fished here for crawdaddies," I told Heracles. "We used string for a line and chewed-up bubble gum for bait."

"Sounds like fun." Heracles smiled at me, then looked at the pond. "When I was around Theo's age I used to come here to sail boats I made myself. They were really beautiful and complicated. They never made it to the other side, though."

"Why not?"

"I rigged up a device that made them explode about ten seconds after hitting the water." Seeing my surprised expression, he said, "Hey, it couldn't hurt anybody, or any other boats, or even a crawdaddy. It just self-destructed."

"But why?"

He shrugged. "Maybe that was the one time the monster inside me got out." Then he looked at Theo, who was throwing stone after stone into the water, faster and faster, harder and harder. I couldn't stand to watch Heracles watching. Spotting a Frisbee in the grass, I picked it up and called, "Theo, want to play with Heracles and me?"

"What're you playing? House? Okay, you're the

mommy and he's the daddy and I'm the widdew baby." He threw back his head and wailed, "Waaaaa!" Several people nearby turned to look.

Exasperated because I still didn't know how to deal with Theo, I threw the Frisbee to Heracles, who tossed it back in a graceful arc. Jumping, I caught it, then threw it. Boy, did it feel good to move like this! I liked watching Heracles move, too, although I felt a little funny about it. Even though I'd seen statues of men in the Metropolitan, and last year this girl Ruthie Rothbart had passed around a calendar with pictures of naked men, I'd never looked at a guy's body with as much interest as I now looked at Heracles's. He had really broad shoulders, a narrow waist, and long legs, and he looked both masculine and graceful.

"My school's got a great Frisbee team," Heracles said.

"A sports team?" I teased him. "You young scientists?"

"Sure. What'd you think, we walked around all day saying 'Eureka'?"

I laughed. "What does *eureka* mean, anyway?"

" 'I've found it.' And you just brought up one of the X-rated parts of science."

"What does *that* mean?"

"The ancient Greek Archimedes figured out the solution to an important problem while he was in the bathtub. He got so excited that he jumped out and ran through town calling *'Eureka!'*—naked."

Another naked man! Flustered, I missed an easy catch. "Don't tell Theo about Archimedes," I said, remembering his mooning me. "He might want to wear an Archimedes costume next Halloween."

Heracles and I kept tossing the Frisbee, talking and

laughing, until we heard a shout. "Smile!" Theo said. "I'm taking *your* picture."

He had my camera. He was looking through the view-finder of my camera.

"Theo, no!" I yelled, running to him. He put the camera behind his back. I wanted to shake him, but it was my voice that shook. "I'm sorry, but I can't let you use that camera. It's old, it's not in the best shape, and it means a lot to me." I held out my palm.

"You think I'm too spastic to take a picture," Theo said.

Before I could say anything, Heracles came between us. "Please, Theo." He also held out his palm. Theo scrutinized his brother's expression. Just as Heracles reached out to take the camera, Theo handed it to me. I cradled it like a baby, then reminded myself that Theo couldn't help behaving like a baby. "Okay, Theo, now I'll take your picture."

"Forget it," Theo said.

"It's a present from Heracles to your father." My voice became insistent. "Do it as a favor, to help your brother and father."

"What are you, crazy?" Theo said. "You want *me* to help somebody? Listen, I *get* help. I don't help anybody."

That shocked me so much, I couldn't say anything.

"Theo, you don't have to do anything you don't want to," Heracles said, his voice gentle. "Come on, I'll make sure you get home all right."

"Shut up! You can't make sure of anything! You can't make sure of one lousy stinking thing!" Theo punched Heracles hard in the stomach, again and again.

*Stop it!* I wanted to scream at Theo. Then when Heracles didn't defend himself at all, I wanted to yell at Heracles, *Do something!*

Theo started to cry. Punching with all his strength, with no response from his brother, he sobbed and gasped and choked.

Heracles grabbed Theo's wrists and held him still. "Theo, are you all right?" His voice was *still* gentle.

With a tremendous burst of energy, Theo wrenched himself from Heracles's grasp, and ran away.

"You can catch him, Heracles," I said quickly.

"He'll go home anyway," Heracles said.

I watched the skinny little figure getting smaller and smaller and smaller. "Here, hold this," I said, handing my camera to Heracles. I ran after Theo.

# 11

"Theo!"

He turned his head, saw me, and kept running. He was so fast—and so reckless. He ran across streets on red lights, darted among cars, taxis, and trucks. I chased him all the way to the deli before I could reach out and grab his jacket, and even then he surged forward, pulling me with him. I had to lunge and tackle him.

Got him! Maybe I wouldn't be a doctor, lawyer, or corporation vice-president—maybe I'd play football with the New York Giants. Standing behind Theo, with my arms around him, I felt his chest rising and falling fast, I felt his little ribs. Wow, was he scrawny! All of a sudden the weirdest feeling came over me—I felt like turning Theo around and hugging him. "Theo?" No answer. "I just thought of a way you can do my portrait."

Turning his head to the side, he said, "You're gonna let me use your camera?"

"No. But you can draw or paint my portrait. I know you like to draw, and I know you're talented."

"Yeah? If you know so much, do you know what I'm supposed to draw or paint with? All I've got are stupid baby crayons."

"I'll give you all the stuff from my drawing and painting classes. I like art, but I'm not that good at it."

There was a long pause, then Theo said, "Know what you're good at?"

Was a kind word coming? A smile maybe? "What?"

"Bull," he said.

I closed my eyes. Getting hold of Theo physically was sure a lot easier than really getting close to him.

"Theo!" Mr. Damaskinakis ran out the deli door. I let go of Theo, who ran into his father's arms. Mr. Damaskinakis held him tightly, murmuring, "My baby . . . my baby."

"Mr. Damaskinakis?"

His expression and his voice hardening, he said, "What do you want, Alexandra?"

"I just want to tell you Theo's all right."

"You think I don't know my boy's all right? Mind your own business, Alexandra."

I flinched, as if he'd hit me. "Wait a minute, I didn't mean—"

He interrupted me. "This is a family thing," he said. He put his arm around Theo, and they walked into the store.

I was standing in the same spot when Heracles arrived a minute later. "Theo's inside with your father," I said.

"Hey, you okay?" Heracles asked, the expression in his eyes concerned.

"Oh, sure. I'm probably just not used to kids, since I'm an only child."

"Heracles!" Mr. Damaskinakis, of course. Heracles handed me my camera, we said so long, he went in the store, and I went home.

The apartment was empty, and a note was taped to the refrigerator:

> Alexandra, see you around five. Don't forget
> our date with Kate and Cary! Love, Mom.

I kind of missed seeing Mom's familiar face and hearing her familiar voice say familiar things—even things like "Did you take out the garbage?" I called Dad, but there was no answer; called Nora, but got her family's answering machine.

Lying on my bed, I thought about Theo, and then about Heracles. When Heracles was lying on his bed, what did he think about? What did he dream about? Becoming a great scientist, so he could make discoveries to prevent problems like his brother's and cure diseases like the one that killed his mother? I wanted to know everything about him—when his birthday was, whether he was allergic to anything, whether he liked Greek foods like stuffed grape leaves. I wanted to know how he felt about me. I fell asleep wondering.

The sound of Mom's key in the lock woke me up, and I scooted out of bed to greet her. "Hi, sweetheart, sorry I'm late," she said. "Would you like to go out to dinner before the movie?"

"Boy, would I! I just realized I'm starving."

"Let's go to a Japanese restaurant," Mom said. "We'll have sushi."

"What is it?"

"Raw fish."

"Ha ha. What is it *really?*"

"Raw fish, cold rice marinated in vinegar, and sea-weed."

Before Mom and I went to the Japanese restaurant, I slipped a plastic-wrapped peanut butter and jelly sandwich into my jacket pocket. At the restaurant I pushed my sushi around my plate and onto my napkin. When Mom went to the ladies' room, I took out my peanut butter and jelly sandwich, rolled it up so it looked like sushi, and ate it with chopsticks.

# 12

Samantha Donaldson was one year old and Oliver Donaldson two. During the couple of hours I was with them, the longest time they spent without moving or making noise was 1.7 seconds. "The Sam and Ollie Show" was crazy, but fun. I hoped the portrait showed it.

It sure was different at Tweed's. His family's apartment was bigger than our old house in New Jersey, and the furniture was right out of the magazines I looked at in the dentist's waiting room. Everything was still and silent. "Where are your parents?" I asked Tweed as we went into the living room.

"Mother's at a concert, and Father's at the club." He gestured toward an elegant chair, and I sat down. "Do you have any brothers or sisters?" I asked.

"An older sister, Tizzie, who's at boarding school." He sat on a chair across from me.

"Is that her real name?" This was the most personal question I'd ever asked Tweed.

"Her name is Elizabeth Tyler Thorpe, but from the time she was a baby her nanny called her Lizzie T. When I came along and tried to say that, what came out was Tizzie."

I smiled at Tweed—a spontaneous, sincere smile. That was the first time I ever heard him say he'd done something imperfectly. It was also the first time he actually seemed nice.

"How about you, Alexandra? Do you have brothers or sisters?"

"Uh-uh. I'm an only child."

"That's typical of today. There are lots of only children living with their divorced mothers."

I couldn't help laughing. "You sound like a TV anchorperson."

His long nose twitched. "I'm just stating a fact."

"But you're talking to a person, and the fact is about my mother and me."

Folding his hands on his knees, Tweed looked like the host of *Masterpiece Theatre*. "That's sort of the point, Alexandra," he began. "What I want to discuss in my term paper is the problem of being an only child with a divorced, career-oriented mother."

I waited to hear what came next.

"I want to ask you how it feels. For instance, how it feels to be alone a lot of the time."

I opened my mouth, but Tweed kept talking.

"And how it feels to be financially insecure—*nouveau pauvre*."

"Uh, Tweed . . ."

"Excuse me, Alexandra. Maybe you don't know

French. *Nouveau pauvre* is the opposite of *nouveau riche*—newly rich. *Nouveau pauvre* refers to women and children who because of divorce are suddenly poor."

"There's something I want to ask you, Tweed."

His eyebrows went up. "Yes?"

"How does it feel to be a *zhlub?*"

"A what?"

"Oh, excuse me, maybe you don't know Yiddish. A *zhlub* is an insensitive, bad-mannered jerk."

As Tweed's mouth opened, I stood up, picked up my camera and coat, and walked out.

I was glad Mom was busy working at her desk when I got home. If she'd stopped for more than a few seconds and really looked at me, she'd have seen how mad I was, and it was too complicated to get into. The phone rang, and I answered it.

"Hello, Ms. Susskind."

"Dad, hi!" Mom waved and left the room, as she always did when Dad called.

"How's it going, babe?"

"Oh, Dad, I really like taking pictures. I've been doing a lot of it." I told him about my favorite photos. "I'll send you a sample this week."

"I'll look forward to that."

"How are you and Wendy?"

"I've started teaching the Kierkegaard course again." Dad wrote his doctoral dissertation on this Danish philosopher Søren Kierkegaard. Now he and Wendy had a cat named Kierkegaard. "Oh and here's some news, Lexie—Kierkegaard's expecting kittens."

"He is?"

We laughed. "She is," Dad said. He cleared his throat.

"And Lexie . . . Kierkegaard's not the only one." He paused. "Wendy's pregnant. Isn't that marvelous?"

I hesitated for just a second. "It's wonderful, Dad. Congratulations. To Wendy too."

"Thanks. The baby's due in late August. Wendy and I are especially pleased about that, because you'll be with us then. Meanwhile, what about helping us find a couple of names?"

"Hmm . . . Kierkegaard's already taken. How does Søren Susskind sound?"

"Silly." We laughed, and talked for a while longer. As always, just before he hung up, Dad said, "Bye for now, babe."

When I hung up, I realized that I wouldn't be Dad's "babe" much longer. I felt a twinge of envy. Dad would be more than a faraway father to the new baby. Then I thought how nice it was that Dad and I not only loved each other, we really liked each other. Besides, I was growing up—I was too old to be anybody's baby anymore.

"Guess what?" I said, as soon as Mom came back in. "Dad and Wendy are having a baby. I never expected that, did you? Dad's old—in his forties—but of course Wendy's a lot younger. Still, isn't it a surprise?"

"It's certainly a surprise to me," Mom said.

"It's true of Kierkegaard the cat also."

"The cat's surprised?"

"No, he's having a baby. I mean, she's having kittens." Laughing at how confused I sounded, I said, "I'm glad for Dad. Wendy too. And I can't wait to see Søren Susskind."

Mom kept nodding, then did a double-take. "Søren Susskind?"

I woke up during the night, and when I went to the bathroom, I saw the light on in Mom's room. At the door I whispered, "Mom, are you awake?"

"No," she said in a normal voice.

Opening the door, I said, "That must be the oldest joke in the world."

"Funny you should mention old. That's what I've been lying here feeling," Mom said. "It just hit me that my child-bearing years are numbered." She laughed. "Sounds dramatic, doesn't it?"

I walked to the bed and sat down on the side. "I didn't know you liked babies so much."

"I don't. You're absolutely right. Thanks for reminding me." Smiling, she said, "Good night, Alexandra."

When I was a little kid, and Mom used to tuck me in, she always kissed me on the cheek and said, "Good night, sweet dreams, I love you." Now I sort of goofed around by pulling her blanket up, bending to kiss her cheek, and saying "Good night, sweet dreams, I love you."

Suddenly Mom's eyes filled with tears. "I love you too," she said. Quickly closing her eyes, she said, "Sweetheart, will you turn off the light?"

"Sure." But first I saw the tears slide down her cheeks.

# 13

Boy, did I have a lot to think about the next day. Mom was on my mind. She was definitely, as Tweed said, "career-oriented." But so what? Dad was too; he loved his work. However, I realized, Dad's work wasn't his whole life. He had hobbies, he'd remarried, and now he and Wendy were even having a new baby. Meanwhile, Mom seemed to be working more and doing everything else less. And she was crying over Dad's kid. If Mom wanted a baby, why did she spend her weekends working? I had the feeling that she was so bummed out by her breakup with Jack Crawford that she'd decided to give up on men and mole out at the office.

Besides Mom, I thought about the portrait of Theo and his portrait of me. As usual, I thought about Heracles, but I also thought about his girlfriend. And who could forget my boyfriend—Osgood Pinhead the Twenty-third, or whatever his name was?

I had so much on my mind that I got halfway home from school before remembering that this was the day I'd planned to develop the portrait of Sam and Ollie. I ran back to school. Luckily, the darkroom was available. I made a contact sheet—one piece of photographic paper showing all the negatives on the roll—so I could decide which negative to print. Using a magnifying glass, I saw the one I wanted. I worked on it right away, and hung it up to dry. Ta-daaaaa! Tomorrow I'd take it right to Mrs. Donaldson. I just knew she'd love it.

Walking home, I had a brainstorm. I decided to give Theo some of my art supplies—without his father's knowing—using Heracles as the go-between. Would Heracles do it? I looked in the deli window and saw him. Unfortunately, I also saw Eleni, standing close to him. It hurt. Even though Heracles and I were just friends, it really hurt. I walked home and called Mrs. Donaldson, who said she was busy tomorrow, could I bring the picture the day after? Sure, I said. Rats, I thought—something else I had to wait for. Then I had to wait for Mom, who came home late again.

The next day, when I looked in the deli window, Eleni had her arms around Heracles's waist. He was slicing ham, not hugging, and he even looked embarrassed, but it was still sort of a hot scene among the cold cuts.

On Wednesday I hurried to the Donaldsons', eager for Mrs. Donaldson's reaction to the portrait. In the elevator I peeked at the print again, and grinned. I rang the doorbell and imagined her smile when she first saw my work.

Mrs. Donaldson frowned. "I don't know what to say, Alexandra."

We were sitting side by side on the sofa, and now I

leaned toward her, keeping my voice calm. "Mrs. Donaldson, professional photographers know that not every client will think every picture is absolutely perfect."

"I hate it," she said.

"Pardon?"

"I'm sorry, Alexandra, but this picture isn't at all what I wanted. Samantha's drooling, and Oliver's pants are drooping." She handed me the picture.

"Hmm . . . yes . . . drooling and drooping. But that stuff's typical of Sam and Ollie, right? Those things happen."

"Many things happen that I wouldn't pay for a picture of, Alexandra."

"Mmm."

"It's not flattering. It's not cute. It's not like any baby picture I've ever seen."

I leaned even closer and looked Mrs. Donaldson in the eye. "Maybe that's because it's *better* than any baby picture you've ever seen."

She stared at me, silently and steadily.

"You don't buy that?"

She shook her head.

"And you won't buy the picture either?"

She shook her head again.

Yuch. I'd never imagined that my picture would be rejected. I felt almost as if I myself were being rejected, but I knew from things Mom said about her own work that professionals did things over—and over and over.

"I'll bring the contact sheet tomorrow, so you can look over all the negatives. If there isn't one you like, I'll take more. I'll keep taking pictures of Ollie and Sam until I take one you want—even if it's their high school graduation picture."

She laughed. "I like your spirit, Alexandra."

"I wish you liked my picture," I said, with a smile. "But I'll try again."

When I got to Damaskinakis's, I wasn't sure I wanted to look in. Who needed any more disappointments? I took a chance, though. No Eleni. Probably she was home shrinking her jeans and sweaters.

I missed Heracles so much, I thought as I watched him. I liked him so much. Looking closer, I laughed. His T-shirt looked like a poster for a 1950s science fiction movie. It showed weird creatures looming on the horizon, and said, Invaders from New Jersey. He saw me and right away came outside.

"Hey."

"Hi."

Both our voices were so high, we could only be heard by each other and dogs.

"Great shirt," I said. "A work of art."

Smiling, he said, "I figured you'd appreciate it. Speaking of art, how's the photography going?"

"Not so artistically. A client just told me she hates my portrait of her kids."

"You're kidding. Got the picture?"

I handed it to him.

"I think it's terrific," he said.

"You do? I'm not alone?"

Shaking his head as he looked right at me, he said, "You're not alone, Alexandra." His eyes were so dark and intense.

I wanted to hug him. Instead, I blurted, "Heracles, I told Theo he and I could trade. He could paint or draw a picture of me and I'd take a picture of him. I also told him I had some art supplies for him."

"What'd he say?" Heracles asked.

"First he made fun of the idea, but then I thought he might be interested, until . . . until your father came out and—"

"And took over," Heracles said.

I nodded. "Your father didn't want me to get involved, because—"

"Because you're not in the family," Heracles said.

"Heracles!" Mr. Damaskinakis called from the store.

I talked fast. "If I give you the art supplies, Heracles, will you give them to Theo?"

He looked in the store, back at me, hesitated. "Yeah."

"Will you remind Theo that we're going to do portraits of each other?"

"Okay." Now he smiled a little.

"Will you . . . will you pick up the art stuff at my apartment at lunchtime on Saturday?"

"Hey, no problem." A big smile.

"Will you get out of my way?"

Eleni was pushing between Heracles and me. Her back to me, she gave Heracles a big kiss on the cheek. Then she turned and greeted me. "How's Osgood?"

"Better than ever," I said.

"Heracles!" Mr. Damaskinakis shouted. Heracles said good-bye, and Eleni wiggled away.

On Thursday I brought the contact sheet to Mrs. Donaldson and held my breath while she looked at it. She found two negatives she liked. On Friday I developed them both and left the prints in the darkroom to dry, planning to pick them up on Monday.

Just after Mom left for the office on Saturday, the

phone rang. "Alexandra? This is Reed. I get the impression I've said something wrong."

"Are you serious?"

"I was just speaking sociologically. I was just summing up . . ."

"I'm just hanging up."

After getting my art supplies together, I got myself together, then looked in Mom's full-length mirror. I saw Alexandra in Wonderland. Tall, thin, with long, straight hair, dressed in a big sweater, baggy jeans, and sneakers —I liked the way I looked.

Heracles must like the way Eleni looked, though, if he'd been going out with her for four years. Could I look like Eleni? I wiggled, then giggled, feeling really silly. I wouldn't want to look like her permanently. But maybe just as an experiment, like Dr. Jekyll trying out being Mr. Hyde?

# 14

I searched through my bureau drawers for the shrunken jeans and the angora sweater that was too small three years ago. The jeans were so tight I had to hold my breath to pull them all the way up and lie flat on my bed to zipper them. It was like an Olympic event—jeannastics. I stood up, and it was hard to breathe. Slipping into the angora sweater, I thought how lucky it was that I was only allergic to dust, mold, pollen, and ragweed. Except I'd never worn angora before . . . "Aaaaachoooo!" Add angora to the list.

I ran to the medicine cabinet for my allergy pills. "Aaaaachoooo!" Since the medicine would take effect in ten or fifteen minutes, and Heracles wasn't due for an hour, I yanked off the sweater and peeled off the jeans, planning to put it all back on later. Meanwhile, I slipped on my favorite old nightgown, which Grandma Susskind had sent from Florida for my twelfth birthday. It used to fall to my ankles, but now it stopped at my knees. It was soft flannel, faded pink, with faded purple flowers. I kept on my knee socks, which had bright red, turquoise, and yellow stripes.

When the doorbell rang, I thought it was the supermarket delivery and I buzzed back. Just as I opened the apartment door, "Aaaaaaaachooooooo!" A sneeze for the Super Bowl of Sneezes. As I opened my eyes, I was still holding a tissue over my nose. "Heracles!"

Uh-oh. This experiment was supposed to show a different side of me, but not this side. It wasn't supposed to show how weird I could look.

"Alexandra, you . . . you look . . . Gotta go," Heracles said.

I closed the door and leaned against it. This experiment showed a different side of Heracles too. Faced with my running nose, he'd run away! What a way to treat a friend. I stood there sniffling, but I wouldn't let myself cry. A few minutes later, I heard the buzzer again. "Doo *did* did?" I asked into the intercom.

"Excuse me?"

I took the tissue from my nose. "Who is it?"

"Heracles."

Completely confused, I buzzed him in and a minute later opened the apartment door. "Here." He handed me a brown bag. "It's soup, from the deli. Careful, though—it's still hot."

I must have looked as surprised as I felt, because he explained, "It's for your cold. Soup steam clears your sinuses, it's a scientific fact."

"Oh, thank you, Heraaaaachooo!"

"How come you didn't tell me you were sick? Why are you even up? Come on, lie down on the couch."

"It's just an allerjaaachoooo!" Heracles led me to the sofa. Trying not to laugh, I lay down. He put the afghan over me and sat in a chair. Then he pulled a napkin, spoon, and container of soup from the bag. As he fed me a spoonful of soup, I started to giggle. It turned into a gargle. Then I started to laugh, but Heracles looked so serious, and so sweet, that I decided to let him baby me.

"Mm. Chicken broth," I said. "It's good."

"Thanks," Heracles answered. "Made it myself, from my mother's old recipe."

"I thought you didn't remember your maaachooo!"

Handing me a tissue, Heracles said, "The recipes are all I remember." I blew my nose. "Excellent tone. I used to play the trumpet, so I know," he said. Holding the spoon halfway between us, he said, "Hey, I just remembered some pictures of my mother. Only I don't remember when or where I saw them."

"Why not ask your father about them?" I said.

"Yeah, sure. Know what he'd say? 'What pictures? We're busy. Get back to work.'"

"You could try," I said.

Ignoring this, Heracles moved the spoon toward my mouth.

Holding up my hand to block the spoon, I said again, "You could try."

"Alexandra . . . here comes the choochoo."

We laughed, and I said, "Uh-oh. Here comes the *ah-choo*. Aaaaachoooo!" More laughing. I sat up. "The soup is delicious. And really powerful—I feel better already." I pulled off the afghan and jumped off the sofa. "Be right back."

In my room I threw off the nightgown and put on my favorite sweater—white wool, soft and pretty—and my favorite jeans, which were straight-legged rather than baggy. My best silver hoops went in my ears. In the bathroom, after washing and drying my face, I saw in the mirror that the medicine had worked—my eyes and nose stayed dry. I put on a little mascara, blusher, and lip gloss, and brushed my hair.

"Hey, are you all right?" Heracles called. "Or are you throwing up?"

"I feel terrific," I called back. My mirror image was glowing. I'm *growing* up, I thought, as I went back into the living room.

"Alexandra, you . . . you look . . ." This was just what he'd said earlier, and right afterward he'd disappeared.

"Don't you dare go away without finishing that sentence!" I said, smiling.

Heracles laughed. "I don't want to go. I want to stay." His eyes shone and his voice sounded like his father's or brother's: "Is somebody gonna *make* me finish that sentence?"

Picking up one of the sofa pillows, I said, "Yeah, me." I threw the pillow at him, and it hit him on the head. Laughing, Heracles threw another pillow at me.

In a minute, all six pillows were being tossed around as Heracles and I tussled on the floor, laughing. A minute after that, Heracles and I were lying on the floor, and we weren't tossing or tussling or laughing. We were kissing. And kissing. And kissing.

It was Heracles who gave me my first kiss, and now it was Heracles I was kissing for the second time . . . and the third . . . and the fourth. I wanted it to go on and on. Wow, was he a good kisser! He must have had a lot of pract—I stopped kissing.

"What's wrong?" Heracles asked.

"I forgot something," I said. "Eleni."

"How about Osgood?" he said.

"Oh, right," I said, sitting up. "I forgot him too."

I wished I'd never made up Osgood. I wished Heracles had never met Eleni. But most of all I wished we'd never started kissing, because now I liked Heracles more than ever . . . and felt worse than ever. I picked up a pillow and threw it on the sofa as hard as I could.

"You're mad at me, right?" Heracles said.

"I'm mad at myself." I threw another pillow, and another. The sixth knocked a picture off the wall.

Heracles got up and hung the picture, then looked at me, his expression thoughtful. Maybe . . . maybe he'd say he wanted to break up with Eleni and go out with me. He bit his lip, put his hands in his pockets. He didn't say anything.

Now I *was* mad. I wanted to hit him with the pillows—or the picture. But even as I thought it, I knew it wasn't fair. He'd been going with Eleni for four years, and he'd only known me for a few weeks. I couldn't expect him to break up with Eleni yet. Maybe someday, though. Someday soon . . .

My smile was shaky as I said, "Want to stay for lunch? We can finish the soup, and I'll make peanut butter and jelly sandwiches." I laughed. "Except I'm probably the only person in New York City who likes peanut butter and jelly sandwiches."

"Peanut butter and jelly sandwiches are my favorite," Heracles said. "You like them too?"

I couldn't believe he said that. "Like them?" I said.

"You know how the eagle's the American symbol, sort of the national bird? I think the pb and j should be the national food."

Heracles laughed. "Yeah. And the American flag should be a white rectangle with two thin stripes across the middle—one brown and one purple."

I laughed even louder than I meant to, then Heracles was so still he seemed to be holding his breath. Softly, he said, "Alexandra, right now I've gotta go, but I'd really like to stay . . . someday soon."

Someday soon! My smile wasn't shaky anymore. Pointing at the coffee table, I said, "There's Theo's art supplies. Tell him to practice for a few days, then we'll figure out when we can do each other's portraits, okay?"

"Right." He was really going to do it. He was going to do something his father wouldn't approve of. And someday soon he'd do something his girlfriend wouldn't approve of—get a new girlfriend. After he opened the door, he turned to me and said, "Listen, I've gotta finish that sentence. You look . . . Alexandra, to me you always look beautiful."

# 15

I smiled for the rest of the weekend. Saturday night Mom took me to see *Potemkin*, a really grim old movie about the Russian Revolution, and I smiled all through it.

Sunday night Mom was working at her desk. I was supposed to be writing a term paper on the poetry of Edgar Allan Poe. Instead, I was tap dancing.

"Alexandra?" Mom looked up from her work. "Will you please stop that? I need to concentrate."

"Sure." I sat on the sofa and opened my lit text. Oh, here was an e. e. cummings poem about spring, with made-up words like "mud-luscious." I said that word out loud and laughed.

"Sweetheart." Mom's forehead was a mass of wrinkles.

"Sorry." I tried to get serious. Then I got to my favorite part of the poem—"when the world is puddle-wonderful." I laughed again.

"Alex . . ."

I stood, dramatically intoned, "Quoth the daughter: nevermore," and swept out of the room. Closing my bedroom door, I twirled around, sank to the floor, and sighed. Mom didn't seem at all happy anymore. I glanced at my notes on Poe's life. One sentence caught my attention: Poe drank too much. I thought, Mom works too much. I remembered a TV news feature about workaholics. Sort of the same way alcoholics got carried away drinking, workaholics overdid working. Mom was becoming a workaholic! What could I do about it? How could I help her?

Tossing aside my textbook, I made a list:

> Things to Do This Week
> (1) Theo—portrait
> (2) Donaldsons—prints
> (3) Mom—workaholic!

Monday morning I got a chance to cross off one item. Walking by Damaskinakis's on my way to school, I saw Theo inside. I waved and smiled, hoping for some sign he'd gotten the art supplies.

He pressed his face against the window, making his features look totally bizarre. Boy, if only I knew how to handle that kid. I motioned for him to come out, then waited. Should I go in, walk on, or what? Finally he ran out, shoved something in my hand, and ran away.

Some papers were stapled together into a comic book. A comic book Theo made! Skimming, I saw that the main character was a tall, blond, skinny teenage girl who carried around a camera, which was actually a gun. She wasn't just shooting pictures, she was shooting bad guys. Wow, Theo was really talented, and he'd worked so hard!

How amazing that he'd made me into his idea of a hero-
ine.

Heracles came out of the store, and my heart soared. I
wished I was wearing pb&j perfume. "Did you see this?"
I handed him the comic. Flipping through it, he grinned.
"Theo's immortalized you."

I looked around. "Where is he? I want to tell him how
much I like it."

"He's on his way to school," Heracles said. "Hey, by
the way, mind if I walk to school with you? There's something I want to tell you." I smiled and nodded, and we
started walking.

"I asked Papa about the pictures of my mother," Heracles said.

"Really? What did he say?"

"He said, 'What are you talking about? We're busy.
Get to work.' "

"I'm sorry, Heracles."

Looking right at me, he said, "I'm glad I tried."

I looked right at him. "You could try again."

He laughed, shaking his head. "I just thought of something," he said. "It's only since the camera was invented
that regular people got to know what their ancestors
looked like."

"That's true. All through history, only rich people
could afford to have their portraits painted," I said. We
kept walking and talking.

As we approached my school, Heracles said, "There's
a great science fiction movie on TV late tonight—the
original 1950s *Invasion of the Body Snatchers.*"

"What's it about?"

"Aliens come into a town, take away people's person-
alities, and turn them into mindless creatures."

Speaking of mindless creatures, Tweed was standing in front of the school building. "Heracles, I have to rush to the drugstore for some film. See you." I walked away, then turned to look at Heracles—who was looking at me.

After school, I took the new prints of Sam and Ollie to Mrs. Donaldson. She liked both. I sold my first pictures! Running into a camera shop, I asked a lot of technical questions, bought filters and film. Now I could afford to take more pictures for myself—pictures for love, besides pictures for money.

Right away, I took one of an old couple jogging past me in identical sweatsuits. Still together after all these years, I thought. Then I laughed. Who said they'd grown old together? Maybe they'd just picked each other up. Nora Nakamura's mother used to read romance novels about heroines who'd loved and lost, but loved again— the Second Chance at Love series. Why not senior citizens' romances—the Last Chance at Love series?

Suddenly I realized that I could take pictures for love in more than one way. Why not take pictures of men that Mom might like? Becoming a workaholic, she'd been avoiding men. I could help her meet some again. I'd make a contact sheet of men in our neighborhood, ask Mom which were the most appealing, and somehow set up meetings. When Mom got involved with a man, she'd stop being a workaholic.

I walked across the street and into an art gallery. "Hi, remember me?" I said to the tall, bearded, fortyish owner. "Last month I sold you a ticket for my school's raffle."

"Yes, I remember you, even though I didn't win the raffle. What are you selling today?"

"Absolutely nothing. Today I'm giving something

away. I'm taking your portrait for free." Then I had an inspiration: I could take these pictures for love *and* money—love for Mom, money for me. "Of course," I went on, "if you like your free sample so much that you want more copies, I can provide them at my usual reasonable rates."

He smiled. "I really don't have time . . ."

"Not even for an aspiring artist?" I said. "Not even for five minutes?" I was already focusing. He laughed. Shoonck.

As I advanced the film, a handsome middle-aged man came in the door carrying a mobile. The owner and the artist greeted each other.

I said to the artist, "As a creative person, you want to encourage creativity in the young, right?" He opened his mouth to answer. Shoonck.

During the rest of the week, I took more pictures of men for Mom. Just for fun I looked for a doctor, a lawyer, and an Indian chief—like the rhyme. I ended up with a psychiatrist, a tax attorney, and an Indian *chef.* The last guy wore a turban instead of a feathered headdress, but he was easy to find: I just walked into a restaurant called Taj Mahal. How could Mom resist a guy who could cook curry and Bombay duck?

I did a lot of other stuff that week. I stayed up late to watch *Invasion of the Body Snatchers,* later the next night to write my Poe paper, late the night after that because Nell Donaldson invited me to her apartment after school and I ended up sleeping over. Nell was nice, even though she didn't like pb&js, just peanut butter sandwiches cut into four squares with the crusts off. Mom thought *I* was a picky eater. When Nell ate Candy Corn, she ate only the white stripe, the one in the middle. She bit off and spit out both ends.

The whole week was fun. But the best part by far was every morning, when Heracles walked me to school. We made each other laugh, made each other think. We were really getting to know each other. He was so nice and smart and funy. How did I live fifteen years without him?

However, by Friday morning, I was overtired. When I was supposed to be meeting Heracles, I was sleeping. Mom had left early and I'd pushed the ten-minute snooze alarm five times. I got to the deli more than half an hour late, never expecting Heracles to be there.

Heracles ran to me and put his hands on my shoulders. "Hey, I was worried about you!"

"I couldn't wake up." I said, yawning and laughing. "I still can't." Heracles's hands were still on my shoulders.

"Listen, Alexandra, you're doing too much stuff. Slow down, take it easy."

Laughing again, I said, "You sound like somebody's mother or father."

"Like my father? Forget it, he'll never slow down."

"And now that I think about it, Mom seems to be moving faster and faster," I said. "Okay, I'll slow down . . . but first I've got to rush to school."

"Alexandra, would you do something for me?"

"Sure, anything," I said. "What?"

"Nothing," he said. "Don't do anything tomorrow. Just goof off."

I thought of how hard Heracles worked. "I will if you will. I mean, I won't if you won't."

"You got it," Heracles said. "I'll pick you up at noon."

# 16

"I'm taking you someplace special, but it'll take a while," Heracles said, when we met in front of my building. "Okay?"

"Sure." Since I was with Heracles, even the subway ride was a pleasure. At one point a man sitting across from us tried to put his own baseball cap on his little son, who pulled it off, saying, "No!" Maybe I should talk to Heracles about standing up to his father, I thought. But then we got talking about other, happier things.

We rode to the Lower East Side, walked down narrow streets, and stopped in front of an old Jewish deli restaurant. "On your day off from the deli, you come to another deli?" I asked, realizing how much I sounded like a New Yorker now.

"If Katz's is just 'another deli,' " Heracles said, "St. Patrick's Cathedral is just 'another church.' " Inside, he pointed at the wall. "That sign's been here since World War Two."

I read out loud. " 'Send a Salami to Your Boy in the Army.' " Somehow I knew the menu wouldn't feature pb&js. I got a foot-long hot dog and a cream soda. Heracles ordered a gigantic pastrami sandwich, with side orders of sauerkraut, potato knishes, pickles . . . and a diet soda. As we started eating, I thought maybe I should mention Heracles's father. But first my mouth was too full, and then we were having too much fun.

Afterwards we walked toward Little Italy. It was sunny and warm, really spring at last. In front of us, a woman walked with her baby daughter, who must have been just learning to walk, because she lurched around like Frankenstein's monster. Watching, her mother beamed.

"You really get along with your mother, right?" Heracles said.

"Sure . . . until recently. I mean, we don't *not* get along now. It's just that we don't see much of each other, and I don't tell her stuff."

"What stuff?"

"Oh . . . how much I like photography. I might even want to be a professional photographer." Until I told Heracles, I didn't know this myself! It was true though.

"What does your mother think you want to be?" he asked.

"What she wants me to be—a doctor, lawyer, or businesswoman. Something that means money, security. I don't blame her. With her liberal arts degree she had to start at the bottom. Last year she was turned down for a promotion, and somebody ten years younger with an M.B.A. got the job."

In Little Italy we looked in the window of a souvenir

shop. "You don't talk much about your father," Heracles said.

"Really? I do have news. He and Wendy are having a baby."

"Hey, what do you think about that?"

"I'm happy for them." I stared at the souvenirs—ways to remember places you only passed through. "Do you think it's weird, Heracles, loving somebody you hardly ever see?"

"Nope. It's not weird at all," he said, looking at me intently.

All of a sudden I felt self-conscious. "Want to know a secret?" I blurted. "I'm finding Mom a man."

"You're kidding." We started walking again. "Uh-uh. I already took pictures of some possibilities. On Monday I'll make a print showing all of them. I'll ask Mom which she likes best, and then I'll get the two of them together."

"Yeah? How?"

"I'll think of something." We looked in a bookstore window, where a book of poems was displayed. "Maybe I'll send Mom a love poem, signed with the guy's name. Know any good love poems?"

Heracles laughed. "I'm a science fiction and horror movie fan. My heroes just grunt or growl or—hey, there's your boyfriend."

"My boyfriend?" I followed Heracles's gaze to the people across the street.

"He just got lost in the crowd."

"It wasn't Osgood, he's at Yale this weekend," I said. "It must've been somebody who looked like him." Was it Tweed? What if Heracles and I really did run into Tweed?

Heracles led me around the corner to another old-fashioned store. "This is a bakery, but it has the best Italian ices in New York," he said.

It wasn't a good old pb&j, but at least it was familiar. I was trying to decide between lemon and cherry when Heracles handed me an ice-filled paper cup.

"Tutti-frutti," he said.

Yuch—fruits and nuts in the ice. I watched as Heracles licked his. I took a tiny lick. Hmm . . . not so bad. We walked outside and sat at a little wicker table that had four chairs, two of them broken. Suddenly I knew what to do so Heracles wouldn't find out that Tweed wasn't Osgood and Osgood wasn't anybody. I'd break up with Osgood. It could also pave the way for Heracles's breaking up with Eleni. In fact, maybe my going with Osgood was one reason Heracles was still going with Eleni. Why hadn't I thought of that before?

"Heracles, about Osgood," I said. "Going with him isn't all good. The only thing he really cares about is the literature of the Middle Ages."

For a second, Heracles's tongue hung suspended on the ice. Then he said, "Listen, don't think going with Eleni is perfect. I could make a bad joke about it. Like, speaking of the Middle Ages, when I'm with her I feel like I'm forty years old and we've been married for twenty."

I kept my voice light. "It's boring, hearing again and again about King Arthur and the knights of the Round Table."

"Know how many nights I've spent hearing about the new round table Eleni's mother bought for their kitchen?"

"It's not easy, hearing Osgood explain Dante's *Divine Comedy.*"

"Hey, could it be worse than sitting in front of the TV while Eleni watches reruns of sitcoms?"

We burst out laughing. Then, just as suddenly, we stopped. We just looked at each other.

"I thought of a love poem," Heracles blurted. "I mean, you asked about one for your mom, right? We had this poem in English class—'How do I love thee? Let me count the ways.'"

"I know that poem. Last year I did a report on the poet, Elizabeth Barrett Browning."

"Yeah?"

"When she was fifteen, she hurt her spine and was supposed to be an invalid for life. Her mother was dead, and her father loved her so much that he kept her close to him and away from everybody else."

"No kidding." Heracles leaned forward.

"She put all her feelings into poetry, and became famous, but she was lonely . . . so lonely."

Heracles was staring at me. "So what happened to her?"

"She reviewed Robert Browning's poetry, and he wrote thanking her. Writing back and forth, they fell in love. But her father said they couldn't see each other." My mouth was suddenly dry, so I stopped to take a lick of my ice.

"And they stopped seeing each other?" Heracles said.

"They eloped to Italy," I said. I took another lick. "She made an amazing recovery, even had a baby. She immortalized her love for her husband in her poems, especially 'How do I love thee? Let me . . .'"

Heracles's eyes fell from my face to his ice, which had melted all over his hand while I was babbling on. I'd better change the subject! "My mother—" I said.

"Right," Heracles said, wiping his hand with a napkin.

"I have to find her a man," I said.

"Wrong," he said, crumpling the napkin and putting it in the ashtray. "That's her job, not yours."

"What?"

He looked directly at me. His eyes were very dark. "Listen, Alexandra, you ought to tell your mother you like photography a lot, maybe want to be a photographer. What right does she have to stop you? You ought to stand up to her."

"What!" I squeaked in surprise. I felt like a doctor whose patient said, "You look lousy, Doc. Take two aspirin and call me in the morning."

"Heracles, that's what I've wanted to say to you. You should tell your father you want to go to Stanford and be a scientist, not work in the store. You should stand up to him."

There were a few seconds of silence and stillness, and then suddenly we were both standing up. At the same time, we said, "Gotta go."

# 17

Heracles and I talked on the way home, but not like before. Probably he was thinking of what I said about his father. I was sure thinking of what he said about Mom. On the subway a woman next to Heracles smacked her little boy on the bottom. *My* mother would never do that, I thought. She never once yelled at me the way Heracles's father yelled at him all the time. So who had the problem parent, Heracles or me?

I was so confused that I made an extra effort to act normal and happy. In front of my building I smiled, held out my hand for Heracles to shake, and thanked him for a very nice day. Right after, I remembered Mom's telling me how her high school hygiene teacher, Sister Immaculata, had taught the girls to end dates. "Put out your hand, smile," she said, "and say, 'Thank you for a lovely time. I owe you nothing.'" Mom and I had laughed about that, but this wasn't funny. Heracles looked as confused as I felt.

The apartment was empty, and a note was taped to the refrigerator: "Alexandra, after I run I'm going to the office for a while. See you tonight." As I threw the note in the garbage, the door opened and Mom came in.

"Alexandra, I met Diana at the office. She's been offered a better job with another company. Do you know what that could mean?"

Couldn't she even say hello? "You could get a new boss?" I said.

"I could *be* the new boss. The new executive editor." Mom's smile was enormous. "As soon as Diana gives notice, I'll campaign for her job. For the next few weeks I'll be leaving home earlier, coming home later, and working more at home too. I hope that'll be temporary, though, and I can settle down some after I get the job—*if* I get the job."

"Uh . . . great, Mom." I tried to smile as broadly as she, but it was hard when my head was spinning.

"Thanks, sweetheart." She was still smiling. "Now, about tonight. How about a French restaurant? We can start with escargots . . ."

"Hold it. I'm taking French, remember? Escargots are snails. Mercy, Mom, mercy."

"You're welcome."

"I'm not saying thank you. I'm begging for a break." This came out with so much feeling that I was surprised, and Mom looked confused. I thought of how confused Heracles looked when I put out my hand and stiffly said so long. Now *I* was confused. "Never mind," I told Mom. "We'll eat what you want. It doesn't matter."

I sort of sleepwalked through the rest of the weekend.

I knew Heracles was right—I should tell Mom I wanted to be a photographer. But I was sure he was wrong to think Mom would try to stop me. All I had to do was tell her, and there was no reaon why I shouldn't. I'd tell her, all right. Not now, though. She was so excited about getting ahead at work. This was no time to spring the surprise that I didn't want to go to the Harvard Business School. I'd tell her soon.

Meanwhile, I avoided Heracles. I didn't want to talk about photography or my mother, and I was pretty sure he didn't want to talk about science or his father. Other than the weather, what could we talk about—Osgood and Eleni?

I woke up on Monday telling myself Mom would be happy when she got that great job, but she'd be even happier when I got her a great guy too. Then she wouldn't be a workaholic anymore. She could enjoy her new job and do it well, without *over*doing it.

After school I made the contact sheet of Mom's men. There were so many nice-looking negatives, I didn't even examine them under the magnifying glass. I was sure Mom would like at least one man. That night after Mom came home from work and we had dinner, I got the contact sheet from my backpack and showed it to her.

"Mom, do me a favor. Tell me which negative you like best. Which guy's most appealing?"

She looked at the paper, and immediately up at me. "Alexandra, why did you take all these pictures of men?"

"Why? I . . . I was experimenting."

"Experimenting with men?" Her eyebrows went way up.

"With photography. Artistic experimentation. I just want to know which portrait you think came out best."

Mom squinted at the pictures for several minutes, then shrugged. "I wish I could help you, but I don't know anything about photography." Handing me the contact sheet, she said, "They all look like good pictures to me, sweetheart. You must be enjoying your hobby."

I gritted my teeth. In my room, I tossed the contact sheet onto my desk, flopped onto my bed, and sighed. No way could I pick out a man for Mom by myself. I had to forget the whole thing. Except, I owed twelve men free samples.

I had to talk to Heracles!

# 18

As soon as I looked in the deli, I saw Heracles and he saw me. Did he hesitate before he came out?

"Hey."

"Hi." I was trying to smile, but I wasn't sure he was, so I stopped. Then I decided he was smiling, or at least trying, so I smiled again, but by that time he'd stopped.

"So what's new?" he said.

"Not much. How about with you?"

He shrugged. "Same old stuff."

I was about to say it was a nice day, when I realized it was gray and dismal. I decided to ask Heracles whether he finished his physics paper. "Did you . . ." I began.

"No, I didn't tell him," he interrupted sharply.

"I didn't mean . . ."

"Did *you?*" This was also fairly sharp.

"Heracles." My voice came out loud. I had to make

myself talk in a normal tone. "I could tell my mother I want to be a photographer any time at all."

"Yeah? So why didn't you?" Heracles folded his arms.

"There's no reason for me to." My voice was getting loud again.

"Yeah right. But there's a reason for me to stand up to my father." His voice was even louder than mine.

I made myself whisper. "My mother doesn't order me around the way your father orders you." Why did my whisper sound like a hiss?

He laughed. "Why should she? You do what she wants without it."

I couldn't believe he said that. I also couldn't believe he laughed at me. Suddenly my hands were on my hips. "That's ridiculous. And who are *you* to tell *me* what to do? How come you're such a wimp with your father and your girlfriend, but you're so bossy with me?"

"A wimp? You think *I'm* a wimp?" Pointing at his muscular chest, he laughed again. "At least I don't spend my whole life with my nose in a book, like Osgood."

"Oh, really? At least Osgood's improving his fine mind. Obviously Eleni spends all her time building her bust. Her chest measurement's bigger than her IQ."

Heracles and I glared at each other, then strode off in opposite directions. Marching toward home, I decided I had to talk to him. What was wrong with him? Why was he acting like such a jerk? But also, what was wrong with me? I'd never talked like that to anybody in my whole life. I was a normal, happy person. "A normal, happy person!" I said. But since I said it out loud, several people passing by looked at me as if they didn't believe me.

I'd show Heracles Damaskinakis how normal, happy, and right I was, and how wrong he was. I'd go right home and tell Mom I wanted to be a photographer. So what if it wasn't the right time? I'd show him how different my mother was from his father. "Mom!" I was so psyched up to tell her, that I called out to her even before I'd opened the door.

The apartment was empty, of course. How could I forget that she'd probably be late again? An hour later she called to say she was sorry, but there was a crisis at the office and she'd be *very* late, so I should just send out for pizza or make myself a sandwich. Again, she said she was sorry.

I opened the refrigerator door, took out the jars of peanut butter and jelly. Uh-oh. There was no white bread. Peanut butter and jelly on pumpernickel? Never. Peanut butter and jelly on Irish soda bread? Since Mom's side of the family was Irish, I gave it a try, but when I tried to spread the peanut butter, the bread turned to crumbs. Then I tried peanut butter and jelly on matzoh, but the matzoh kept cracking. Oh, no, both sides of the family were letting me down! Peanut butter and jelly on a croissant? How did you say "yuch" in French? Back to pb&j on pumpernickel. It satisfied my stomach, but not my soul.

When Mom finally got home, I'd managed to psych myself up all over again, but she looked so tired I couldn't go through with it. Instead, I set my alarm for early the next morning, and had coffee and toast ready for her when she woke up. "I thought we should have some time to talk," I said.

"Alexandra, what a sweet, thoughtful thing to do." She hugged me, and we sat at the table. Then she started talking about all the problems at work, starting with the president of the company and working down to a new file clerk. "You know the book *The Lord of the Flies?* Well, this man is so overbearing everybody calls him the Lord of the Files." While I was laughing, she got up and started putting the dishes in the sink.

"Mom, there's something I . . ."

She'd already turned on the faucets. "What did you say?"

When she turned them off, I said, "Could I talk to you for a minute?"

"Sure, but I have to rush to get to an early meeting. Come and talk while I'm getting ready."

I followed her right into the bathroom. I could talk all right, but since she was taking a shower, then brushing her teeth, then blow-drying her hair, she couldn't hear. Finally, I followed her into her room, sat on her bed, and spoke out loudly and clearly.

"Mom, I really like taking photographs."

"Mm, I know. Oh, dear, my last pair of panty hose has a run."

"I like it so much I want to be a photographer."

"I'll just have to pick up a new pair on the way to work." After buttoning her blouse, she smiled at me. "It's a wonderful hobby, although it is expensive."

"Not for a hobby."

"Alexandra, you just reminded me," she said, stepping into her skirt. "My bank is sponsoring a seminar for young women interested in careers in banking and finance. I signed you up."

She whipped on her jacket, then sat next to me and put on her socks and running shoes, so she could walk the twenty blocks to the office. Putting her arm around me, she said, "Thanks for getting up with me. I appreciate the breakfast . . . and I loved our talk." She kissed me on the cheek and left the room.

"Mom!" I called, jumping up. "Mom, I have to tell you something!"

She came back in and smiled at me. "What is it, my darling daughter?"

My mouth opened and closed a couple of times. Finally I said, "You forgot your attaché case." As I handed it to her, I thought for a second about dropping it on her foot.

When she left, I sat on her bed, looking like the sculpture *The Thinker*. A few minutes later, the phone rang.

"Alexandra? It's Heracles. Hey, I'm sorry. I didn't mean . . ."

"Neither did I. I'm really sorry too. I . . ."

"Listen, can I walk you to school this morning? There's something I want to tell you."

# 19

"You were right," I said to Heracles as soon as I came out of my building and saw him standing there in his red hooded jacket. "I should stand up to Mom."

"You were right too," he said. "About Papa."

This time I didn't wait to see if he was smiling, I smiled at him. "Boy, am I glad you called."

As we started walking, he said, "I want to tell you why I didn't tell Papa."

I laughed. "Wait till you hear how tough it was trying to tell my mother. She went into a *mom*ologue about her job. To get her attention I'll have to call her secretary for an appointment."

"Alexandra, you don't understand. I want to tell you why I *can't* tell Papa." He took a deep breath. "I was thinking about telling him, I really was. I was thinking about how and when I could say it. Then I remembered something, something else about my mother . . . and Papa and Theo . . . about my whole family. It happened just a couple weeks before my mother died." He looked at me. "If you don't want to hear it . . ."

"If you want to tell me, I want to hear it."

We walked another block before he went on talking. "My mother'd been in and out of hospitals for a long time, and was lying on the couch, weighing . . . I don't know, she probably weighed less than I did then, less than Theo does now. I was in my room, studying, like always." He bit his lip, hard. "The thing is, Alexandra, I was studying and hiding. I didn't want to look at her. She was dying, and I couldn't stand it, and I couldn't do anything about it."

"Heracles, that's horrible. And you were only ten years old?"

He didn't answer, and he kept looking straight ahead, not at me. "All of a sudden I heard Theo, who was only four, saying, 'Papa, when Mama was alive . . .' I heard Papa gasp and say, 'What are you saying, you stupid boy?' I heard him slap Theo hard." Heracles winced, as if he were the one being slapped. "I ran in. I could see Papa from the back, looking down at Theo. His face had a red spot from Papa's big hand. Theo was shaking all over, and Papa . . . Papa was crying. I couldn't see it, but I could hear it. Mama was on the couch, with her eyes open, seeing and hearing everything, not able to do anything."

"Oh, Heracles."

"I took Theo to my room and calmed him down. Then I came out and told Papa he'd be getting more rest, because I wanted to start helping him in the store after school and on weekends."

We walked blocks without saying anything. Finally I said, "So you've been calming down your brother and helping your father ever since?"

Heracles didn't answer. We were practically at my school. I spoke softly. "Heracles, do you think you have to do that for the rest of your life, even though your father and brother aren't even nice to you?"

"You don't understand, Alexandra. I'm not doing it for them. I'm doing it for Mama. It's what she would have wanted."

The school bell rang, but I stood still, looking at Heracles. Raindrops started coming down, but I stayed there. I almost kept my mouth shut, but then I had to say, "How can you be sure it's what your mother would have wanted, if that's all you remember of her?"

He didn't say anything. "Maybe if you asked your father about those pictures, they'd bring back happier memories of your mother," I said.

"Yeah, and what if they didn't? What if they brought back memories like that one, or worse? Who'd have to live with those memories, Alexandra, you or me?"

I flinched. "You're right." The rain was coming down harder now. "Who am I to tell you what to do? I couldn't even tell my mother I want to be a photographer. I'm afraid she's become a workaholic. She doesn't want to do anything but work, and she wants me to do nothing but work—her kind of work. I don't want to think about it, much less talk to her about it and tell her I don't want a life like hers." Shaking my head, I said, "Boy, my life's a lot less simple than it used to be."

"Yeah, mine too," Heracles said. "Maybe you were better off before I told you to stand up to your mother."

"Maybe things were better for you before I said you

should stand up to your father. Are you sorry you tried to tell him? Are you sorry it made you remember?"

He didn't say anything for a long time. He didn't even put up his hood. The rain was soaking us both. "I'm not sure," he said.

"I know what you mean. I'm not sure about anything anymore," I said, and we turned away from each other.

For the rest of the day I threw myself into my school-work like never before. In history class I denounced King George III as if I'd actually experienced taxation without representation. In chemistry class I pushed Mr. Horowitz into a debate about clones, taking a fiercely anticlone position. In art class Mrs. Attanasio went around telling everybody their charcoal sketches were too neat and pre-cise, everybody should let go and open up. "More feel-ing," she said, as she looked over kids' shoulders. "More feeling." She looked over my shoulder at the black swirls that filled the whole page. "Less feeling," she said.

After school I started developing the free samples of Mom's men. As I looked at the contact sheet under the magnifying glass I thought something was weird. When I'd first looked at the sheet, I must have been concentrat-ing on the men, because now I could see problems with a lot of the pictures—a loafer sticking out of the edge of one, a pair of khaki pants, the sleeve of a tweed jacket . . .

A tweed jacket, khaki pants, and loafers? How come Tweed Thorpe the Fourth was lurking around in my pictures—and my life? I quickly got my things together, opened the door—and smashed into Tweed.

# 20

"Are you following me?" I shouted.

"Not at the moment," he said, flat on his back.

"Tweed, you've been following me so you can report on my life in your stupid term paper, right?"

At first he just stared at me. Then he said softly, "I haven't meant to insult you. I'm truly truly sorry."

When he struggled to get up, I held out my hand to help him. "I'll accept your apology if you promise you won't follow me again."

Holding up his hand, Tweed said, "I solemnly swear."

I shook my head. Could I ever understand Tweed? "Tweed," I said, "if you can think of some better questions, we can try that interview again."

"Only if you'll take my portrait," he said.

Smiling at each other, we agreed to meet at his house after school the next day. I went back inside the darkroom and got so absorbed in developing the pictures that I didn't get home until six thirty.

Mom was already at her desk, papers piled high. "Sweetheart, you're late," she greeted me.

I meant to say "I'm sorry" but "No kidding" came out.

"Alexandra, do you have a problem?"

"Me?" I pointed at myself and shook my head. "Never." Hanging up my jacket, I saw Mom looking at me oddly, so I did my best to make casual predinner conversation. "I saw a cockroach in the bathroom this morning."

"Oh . . . well . . . did you kill it?"

"No, I'm holding it hostage." I went to my room. A few minutes later, Mom knocked on the door, but I grunted that I was doing my homework, and after a minute of silence she went away.

As I walked to Tweed's the next day, his home and mine did seem far apart. Park Avenue was a gleaming gray-white, clean and serene. Tweed's life must be so different from Heracles's and mine, I thought. I was trying to decide whether to spill my guts about growing up as an only child of a single, career-oriented woman. I could sum up by saying it had been fine so far, but I had the feeling that when I turned sixteen in a couple of weeks I'd be getting a birthday memo instead of a birthday card.

I didn't have to decide, though, because as soon as Tweed and I sat down, he said, "I'm not going to write about you, Alexandra."

"You're not?" I asked, surprised. "After you went to the trouble of following me? Why not?"

"Well, as I've followed you, I've . . . I've grown to . . . to admire you."

Surprised, I watched Tweed push his hair from his forehead. "Besides admiring you," he said, "I've become sort of . . . attached to you."

Now I was amazed. "You have?"

He nodded. "Even though you're involved with that Greek grocer's son."

"We're not sure we're involved with each other," I said.

"Then will you go out with me Saturday night?"

Tweed looked so eager. Could it possibly be fun to go out with him? It certainly would be different. Oh, why not try it? Let Mom be a workaholic and Heracles a martyr, I might as well be happy.

During the rest of the week I finished the free samples of Mom's men, and got orders from three guys for more pictures. I hung out after school again with Brooke, who I found out liked cream cheese and jelly sandwiches, and Dana, who it turned out liked peanut butter and banana on whole wheat bread. I called Nora, and she said she was in love with a Chinese boy named Henry Fong, who, as the star of the school wrestling team, was known as King Fong. Dad called me to say that Kierkegaard had kittens, which he and Wendy named after philosophers— Socrates, Plato, Martin Buber, and Jean-Paul Sartre. Then Saturday night Tweed and I went out.

Tweed did everything to make it a great date. Of course he wore his tweed jacket, but he also got especially duded up with a nice shirt and tie. He took me to a fancy East Side restaurant and then to a play. To top it off, he actually took me home in a cab.

The only problem was, when I saw Tweed all dressed up I thought of how funny Heracles's Invaders from New Jersey T-shirt was, and how fantastic Heracles looked in his red hooded sweatshirt. The play was boring, but Tweed explained it was supposed to be boring because it was about boredom. I thought of how exciting it was to watch *Dr. Jekyll and Mr. Hyde* with Heracles. And when our fancy dessert, called *gelato*, turned out to be a lot like Italian ice at twice the price, I thought of how much fun Heracles and I had on the Lower East Side and in Little Italy.

After we got out of the cab, I covered my mouth as I yawned. "Thanks for a lovely evening, Tweed," I said, putting out my other hand.

"That's what they all say," Tweed said. "Every girl I've ever taken out."

"I'm really sorry, Tweed."

"And I've taken out every kind of girl—every height, weight, race, religion, astrological sign . . ."

"Including girls who live on Park Avenue?"

"They're the only ones I ignore," Tweed said. "Those debs are so boring."

I bit my lip to keep from laughing, but I knew my eyes showed how I felt. Tweed stared at me for a few seconds, then did something really incredible. He laughed at himself. I laughed too—not at him, with him, and with affection. "Tweed, will you tell me something?"

"The secret of my sex appeal?"

Smiling, I shook my head. "Isn't it nice being rich?"

"Are *you* interviewing *me* for *your* social studies paper?"

Laughing, I denied it.

"Well, I don't have some of the problems most people do, but I have some others most people don't."

"Like what—you have so much money in your pockets it makes your pants fall down? Name one problem."

"Living up to my name," he said instantly. "And it's no joke."

"I'm sorry," I said.

"I remember once you said, 'I'm not another anybody.' But I am. I'm Reed Thorpe the Fourth, and I come from a long line of very successful people. For me to be successful is expected, I get no credit for it. The only way I could get attention would be to fail."

As I was thinking about that, Tweed said, "I've failed with you, haven't I?"

"Nope. You've succeeded in making me like you a lot." We smiled at each other. I said, "Can I ask you one more thing?"

"You want to ask me to kiss you good night, don't you?"

"Do you like being called Tweed?"

"I loathe, despise, and abhor it," he said.

I held out my hand. "Thanks for a great date, Reed."

Even though on my date with Reed I kept thinking of Heracles, I reminded myself afterward that there were other boys I could date. The trouble was, I soon found out, every time I looked at any boy, I thought of Heracles. Any time I looked at any girl, I also thought of Heracles. With my eyes closed, lying in bed at night, I thought of Heracles. Could he be thinking of me? If he was, why didn't he tell me?

Over the next week or so, I flirted with a couple more boys, hung out with some girls, talked to Nora and Dad, took pictures, wrote papers, cooked dinners—just like a normal, happy person. I didn't talk to Mom, but she was around so little, she didn't even notice that I wasn't speaking to her. She didn't know her darling daughter was getting madder and madder at her.

Then one afternoon I started taking pictures, and when I realized it was late evening, I called Mom to apologize for worrying her. She wasn't home yet. This was it, I decided. This was the night to stand up to Mom and tell her off. I was concentrating on it so hard that I forgot to avoid the deli, and then I couldn't stop myself from peeking in. I saw Heracles. Right away, I knew something was wrong.

# 21

Heracles was really pale, and there were dark circles under his eyes. He was at a cash register, and there was a long line of customers waiting to be checked out; nobody was at the other cash register.

I quickly walked inside and went over to him. "What's wrong?" I whispered.

He glanced at me, then went back to ringing up sales. "Papa's sick."

"He's gonna die!" Theo yelled, popping up from under the counter.

"Papa's not going to die. I've told you a million times, Theo," Heracles said softly. "It's probably just the flu. It'll be over in twenty-four hours if he can get some rest."

"Liar," Theo said. Taking a rubber band from the counter, he shot it at Heracles, and raced through the store. Customers watched him, some frowning, others nudging each other or raising eyebrows.

"You're not lying, are you?" I asked Heracles.

"I don't lie," he said, and I felt a pang. I'd lied a lot lately. Helping him bag groceries, I asked, "Where's Eleni?"

"Her sister had a baby a couple days ago. She's been home taking care of her sister's other kids. She'll be back tomorrow."

"Heracles, you stayed home from school today, didn't you? You've been working here alone since seven this morning. I can tell."

"So?" Heracles said. He handed a bag of groceries to a customer, and right away began ringing up the next customer's order.

"Why don't you ask some of your relatives to come over and take care of your father or Theo or help out in the store?"

"Papa won't stand for it."

"Why not close the store early?"

Heracles just laughed.

"Okay, so your father won't stand for that, either. Are you going to work until midnight, with Theo running around?"

Heracles turned to the next customer. "Yes, sir?"

Theo ran toward the stairs to the apartment. I ran after him. He got to the top of the stairs before I grabbed his shirttail and stopped him. His back to me, he said, "Pop's dead, isn't he?"

"Of course not. He's a healthy man. But we have to let him sleep." I tried to take Theo's hand, but he resisted. I practically dragged him down the stairs and through the store to Heracles, who was helping one customer while a couple waited. "I'm taking Theo home with me," I whispered.

"Are you nuts?" Heracles whispered back.

"I'll bring him back tomorrow. If you need anything before then, call me." I dragged Theo to the door. As I opened it, several more customers came in. Theo belched. If King Kong had belched, it wouldn't have been as loud.

At that second, I remembered Mom's needing peace and quiet so she could work at home. I stood still. Telling her off was one thing, unleashing Theo on her was another. I wasn't quite that mad at her, and I didn't want her mad at me. Then I looked at Heracles, who seemed so strong, but was now so pale. I looked at Theo, who seemed so tough, but was trembling.

As I opened our apartment door, my heart was pounding, I was sweating, and I was biting my lip. Mom turned around. Who knew what she'd say or do? I only knew what I had to do.

"Mom, this is Theo Damaskinakis. His father's sick in bed, and Heracles is working by himself until midnight in the deli. So I've brought Theo home to . . . to spend the night."

Mom opened her mouth, but no sound came out.

"Hey, lady, pick a nose," Theo said.

"Never mind," I quickly told him. I talked just as fast to Mom. "Don't worry, we'll stay in my room and be so quiet you won't even know we exist." Turning back to Theo, I tried to sound cheerful. "Let's go to my room. Want to sleep in my bed? Or in my sleeping bag?"

"Let's both sleep in your sleeping bag," Theo said.

I took his hand and pulled him to my room, closing the door. Boy, did I want to crawl into bed—or under it.

Theo sat on the bed, then bounced. Ignoring this, I

smiled at him. "Theo, thanks for giving me that comic book. I loved it. You did a great job."

"Took you long enough to say so," he said, now standing on the bed.

"You're right, and I'm sorry." Trying to get his attention, I pointed at my chessboard. "Want to play chess? If you don't know how, I could teach you. I used to belong to my school's chess club."

"They let you in a chest club?" Theo said. "What for—to build yours up?" Now he was jumping on the bed.

"Chess, not chest," I shouted. I covered my mouth, remembering that I'd told Mom there wouldn't be any noise. "Don't jump on the bed," I whispered.

He stopped jumping, sat, and started bouncing. "Theo, don't bounce on the bed," I said.

Standing on his head, he put his feet against the wall. When he took them away, there were sneaker tracks, as if somebody had walked on my wall.

"Get off the bed," I said. "But don't sit at my desk," I quickly added, as he pulled out the desk chair and picked up my homework. "Why don't you sit on . . . on the floor?"

"What do I look like, your pet?" He got down on all fours and crawled, growled . . . and roared.

"Shhhhhh!" Mom had to have heard him.

Theo got up. "What's in here?" He opened the top drawer of my bureau.

"Nothing," I said. My underwear was in there. He held up a pair of panties. "Give me those." I grabbed them.

Reaching in the drawer, he pulled out a bra. "Hey, what's this?" It was the kind of bra that hooked in the front. He draped it over his head so one cup was on each side. "Earmuffs?" he said, then started laughing like a loon.

Desperate to shut him up, I clamped my hand over his mouth. He bit me. I screamed, as much in shock as in pain. Seconds later, Mom was at the door. "Alexandra!"

"Sorry for the noise it's all right now just go back to work," I said in one breath.

She came in anyway.

"Everything's under control," I said, my voice very high and fast. "Everything's normal, everything's happy. I can take care of everything." I glanced at Theo, who still had my bra on his head. "I can take . . ."

"Alexandra," Mom said.

"I can . . ." I started again. Then I closed my eyes. "I can't," I whispered. I burst into tears. "Mom . . . help!"

# 22

Mom put her arm around me. "Sweetheart, I'll take care of it." Her arm felt strong, her voice sounded calm and sure.

"But you have work to do," I said.

"This is the work I have to do right now."

"Mom . . . you don't know Theo," I said.

Theo's eyes were more enormous than ever, and his fists were clenched. Mom could never handle him in a million years.

She turned to him. "Alexandra and I are delighted to have you with us, Theo—if you behave yourself. Biting's definitely not behaving." Her voice still calm and sure, she said, "I'll bet you have some medicine that helps you behave, right?"

"I forgot it," Theo said. "Big deal. I always forget it. Pop does too."

"Alexandra, will you please go to Theo's house and ask his brother for the medicine?" Mom said. "Meanwhile, Theo and I will get acquainted."

I ran out of the apartment. When I came back, I couldn't hear a sound coming from it. What place was silent with Theo around? Did he jump out the window? Did Mom push him? Did he push Mom?

When I opened the door, I saw Mom at her desk, working. "Where's Theo?" I asked.

"In your room, drawing," she said. "We should leave him there until the alarm rings. I told him I'd read him a good-night story, but first he had to amuse himself quietly for fifteen minutes. He set the alarm himself." She went back to her work. I flopped onto the sofa and closed my eyes.

The alarm rang, and Theo ran into the room. "I did it!" he yelled to Mom. "Told you I could."

Smiling, Mom said, "You were absolutely right. I'll bet tomorrow you can amuse yourself quietly for *twenty* minutes."

"Bet I can," Theo said. "Now you're gonna read me a book, right?"

"Absolutely right again. But first, your medicine." Mom gave it to him, and he took it without protest. "Sit on the couch, please, Theo. I'll sit next to you. But you have to sit still—no squirming—while I read." She went to my room and brought out one of my favorite childhood books, *Where the Wild Things Are*, by Maurice Sendak.

"Forget it, that's a baby book," Theo said.

"In a way," Mom said. "But there's something about this book that I love, and I'm a grown woman. Tonight,

Theo, I need to read this book—not just to you, but to me. I hope you'll understand."

Theo looked at her as if she were crazy. "Don't give me that crap," he said. "Grown-ups don't need anything. And they don't read baby books."

"You have a choice," Mom said calmly. "Do you want to listen to me read this book, or do you want to get ready for bed?"

Theo hesitated, snorted, and said, "Listentoyouread."

"Excellent choice," Mom said. She opened the book and read with great feeling. It brought back all the times she'd read to me. When she got to the part where the hero, Max, goes to where the wild things are, Theo began wiggling around.

Mom closed the book. "I can't concentrate when you fidget. If you want me to finish, you have to sit still."

"I can't," Theo said.

"I think you can," Mom said. "I think you can do a lot, Theo, especially if you take your medicine and stick to your diet."

Theo chewed on a fingernail, scratched his nose, cracked his knuckles. "I'll try to sit still."

"Good," Mom said, smiling at him. She opened the book and read so beautifully that Theo seemed mesmerized. Just before the end, I quietly got up and got my camera.

"'. . . where he found his supper waiting for him,'" Mom read, "'and it was still hot.'" Shoonck. Neither of them even noticed me.

"Read it again," Theo said. Mom looked at him and smiled, but didn't say anything.

"Please?" asked Theo. Wow, what a first!

"I'll read it once more tonight, if you wash your hands

and face, brush your teeth, and get undressed and into bed in fifteen minutes."

"I'll set the alarm," Theo said, but he didn't get up. He glanced at Mom, looked away at the wall of books. In the mildest voice I'd ever heard from him, he said, "I'm a wild thing."

"Everybody's a wild thing some of the time," Mom said. "But we learn to stop, to come back from where the wild things are."

"I can't," Theo said, in a very small voice.

"You stopped tonight, Theo. You drew quietly for fifteen minutes, and you sat still for even longer while I read the book. That's two victories. Two triumphs."

Theo's mouth started to sneer, but his eyes were shining. "What's that word—triumph? How do you spell it?"

Mom told him. "Congratulations on your two triumphs," she said. Theo went off to get ready for bed.

Now it was my voice that was mild. "How'd you know how to deal with Theo, Mom?"

She was looking at the cover of the book. "I worked with kids like Theo in a clinic one summer."

"I didn't know that."

"There may be one or two things I haven't told you about myself," Mom said softly, with a smile.

I hesitated, then asked, "Mom, do you think if you'd been Theo's mother, he might not be so . . . he'd behave differently?"

"Differently? Yes. Better? Who knows?"

We sat there together without saying anything. Mom traced with her finger the figures of the wild things, who actually looked lovable.

The alarm rang. "I'm in bed!" Theo called.

Mom and I looked at each other. "Three triumphs," I whispered, and she nodded.

"Dammit, I said I'm in bed!" Theo yelled.

# 23

The next morning Mom didn't rush off to work early. She stayed and sort of supervised Theo. She was wonderful. Maybe she wasn't even a workaholic anymore. Maybe she'd snapped out of it, the way she'd snapped out of all that crying. While Theo was washing up, I helped Mom set the table for breakfast. "Mom, thanks for taking care of Theo."

"I like Theo," she said, setting down glasses for juice. "And I'm fairly confident about handling emergencies, ever since I took that office crisis-management course.

"Which reminds me," she went on, "I was supposed to finish a report last night, so I'll be staying late tonight to do it. I probably won't get home until after you're asleep."

She was wonderful, but she was also a workaholic. I wanted to cry from disappointment, but I just let my shoulders slump.

When I brought Theo back to the deli, Mr. Damaskinakis was behind the counter. Seeing his father, Theo ran and threw his arms around him so hard he almost knocked him over. Mr. Damaskinakis closed his eyes and rocked his son from side to side. I was about to leave when Theo reached out to grab some candy from the counter. Mr. Damaskinakis saw him, but let him.

My shoulders slumped some more. I left the store and started for school. "Alexandra!" Heracles was running after me. "Hey, thanks for taking care of Theo," he said, catching up.

I looked at every feature of his great face before I answered. "You're welcome. But Mom's the one who did it."

"How? Karate?"

"She once worked in a clinic with kids like Theo. She made him take his medicine and stick to his diet, she told him what the rules were and only rewarded him when he followed them."

Heracles was nodding. "Theo's teachers keep telling Papa to do those things, but he can't . . . or won't." Heracles looked right at me, his eyes shining. "Alexandra, I talked to Papa a little," he said. "Early this morning, I asked him again about the pictures. Look what he gave me." Heracles pulled an envelope from the back pocket of his jeans. Very carefully, he took out a faded snapshot and passed it to me.

I held it in my palm, as if it were a living thing. It showed a young woman, tall and broad-shouldered, with black hair and eyes, and high cheekbones, standing at a kitchen table, stirring something in a pot. Next to her was a little boy, standing on a chair, stirring something in his own little pot. The woman and the boy were smiling.

"Oh, Heracles, your mother's so beautiful, and you both look so happy."

"That's just what I thought." Heracles spoke quickly, his eyes becoming even brighter. "I used to remember Mama looking like that 'Migrant Mother,' but maybe she only looked so sad when she was sick."

"You look like her," I said.

"Yeah, I do." Smiling, shaking his head, he said, "This is probably nuts. Promise you won't laugh."

"I promise."

"You think maybe it was because of Mama that I got involved in science? I mean, here I was, mixing stuff up, kind of experimenting." He didn't wait for my answer. "There's one thing the picture did get me to remember: it was Mama who made me think I could be a scientist. She was the one who told me I was smart."

"What a great thing to remember."

"And that made me remember something else. Come here, I'll show you." He led me back toward the deli, and pointed at the sidewalk, where two big letters were scrawled in the cement. "My initials," he said. "I put them there when I was so little, I made my *D* backwards." Laughing, he said, "Now I even remember doing it. Papa was busy in the store—naturally. If he'd seen me, he wouldn't have let me go through with it. It was Mama who laughed and said, 'Go ahead, go ahead.' "

"Your mother told you to make your mark," I said. "Another great thing to remember."

"Maybe Mama would've understood my wanting to go to Stanford. Maybe she would've encouraged me," Heracles said. "Alexandra, I'm going to tell Papa I want to be a scientist."

"I'm so glad," I said, a smile filling my face.

"So how about you?" Heracles said.

My smile disappeared. "I tried to tell Mom, but—"

"When at first Papa wouldn't tell me about the picture, you're the one who told me to try again," Heracles said.

I sighed. "Heracles, I really think no matter how many times I try to tell Mom, she'll be too busy to listen."

"There's got to be some way to get her attention."

"I could call her secretary for an appointment."

"You're kidding, Alexandra, but maybe you really have to do something weird like that," Heracles said. "The only way I got Papa to talk was when he was flat on his back in bed, too weak to work. It was like his world was upside down, he was totally off guard."

I started to shake my head, but Heracles looked so serious. I thought about what he said. Seconds later, I grabbed his arm. "Heracles, I just thought of a way to turn Mom's world upside down."

"What is it?"

"Heracles!" his father called.

"It's too weird . . ." I said.

"Heracles!" yelled his father.

I let go of Heracles's arm. He grabbed my shoulders. "Alexandra, whatever it is, do it."

"Heracles!"

"I'll do it," I said.

# 24

The next morning Mom knocked on my bedroom door. "Sweetheart, I'm leaving very early today, but I wanted to wake you first." She opened the door. Then she opened her mouth.

I was at my desk, studying. Books were piled around me, a pencil was behind my ear, and a row of pens was in the pocket of my pajama top. "The early bird gets the A's," I said.

"Alexandra, I'm impressed," Mom said.

"I hoped you'd be," I replied, then dove back into my books.

That evening, when Mom came home, she called out to me as she opened the apartment door. "Sorry I'm so late. I hope you had din—"

She saw me at *her* desk, studying. "I hope it's okay," I said. "Your desk holds so much more." This time the books were piled even higher.

"You certainly have a lot of work," Mom said, putting down her attaché case. "Did you eat dinner?"

Rummaging among books and papers, I produced part of a pb&j.

"That's not very substantial." Mom took off her jacket and hung it up. "I'm hungry too. Let me see what's in the freezer."

She went to the refrigerator, opened the freezer door, and stared inside. Then she closed the door and did an abrupt about-face. "Alexandra, what's in the freezer?"

"Uh . . . you mean, besides the frozen broccoli?"

Mom said, "Did you ever see me react this way to broccoli?"

"Nope," I admitted. "*I* react that way to broccoli. You actually like broc—"

"Alexandra . . ."

"It's my science project, Mom." She just stared at me. "It died and I froze it," I explained, "instead of using formaldehyde." She kept staring. I explained further. "I plan to dissect it."

"I see," she said. Her face was as white as the refrigerator.

"Bet I get an A," I said. "It's pretty original—dissecting a gerbil."

"It certainly never occurred to me," Mom said. She closed her eyes and shuddered, then opened her eyes and sort of pulled herself together. "Alexandra, sweetheart, I'd like my desk back—and please don't ever dissect anything on it. But I must say, your ambition is admirable."

"Thanks, Mom. I was just following your example," I said. I smiled at her and she smiled back, although a bit shakily.

The next night when Mom came home I was in my room. She apologized for being late as she knocked on the door. Opening the door, she said, "Anything interesting happen today?" She looked around, first quickly, then slowly. "Alexandra, what's happened to your room?"

"I turned it into an office," I said, from my desk. "My schoolwork's my job."

Mom stared at the blackboard that almost covered one wall. Boy, was I lucky my school was about to throw out this old stuff.

Picking up a pointer, I indicated the geometry problems I'd written on the blackboard. "Fascinating, huh?"

Mom didn't answer. She stared at the next wall, on which there was a large map of the world. I pointed at it. "The pushpins show trouble spots around the world that we're studying in current events class."

Nodding, she looked beyond. I said, "This file cabinet's for term papers, notes, old tests . . ."

"Very businesslike," Mom said.

"Am I your daughter or not?" I said. "I was born to go to the Harvard Business School."

Mom's forehead got really wrinkled. She shook her head, and it was a minute before she said anything. "Speaking of the day you were born, Alexandra, your sixteenth birthday is coming up. What would you like for a present?"

"Guess," I said, grinning.

"Well, last year you wanted tapes . . . the year before, clothes . . ."

"Mom, I'd really like an attaché case."

"But you have a backpack for your books."

"My backpack makes me feel like a schoolgirl. I want to feel like a businesswoman. Just like you."

"That's touching," Mom said, and smiled—sort of.

Mom and I went to a Thai restaurant on Friday night. As she unfolded her napkin, she said, "Together at last, Alexandra. We've hardly had a minute to talk this week."

I removed my pencil from behind my ear, grabbed a napkin, and started scribbling. "Excuse me, Mom. I just got an idea for a poem for English class." A few minutes later I was still writing.

"Sweetheart, I'm glad you're working so hard at school, but you should really stop and eat something," Mom said, handing me my chopsticks.

I took them without looking up. I got confused, though. I stuck one chopstick behind my ear, tried to write with another, and tried to eat with my pencil. When I looked up at Mom, she looked worried.

Going into the living room on Sunday morning, I saw Mom eating a bagel while working at her desk. She saw me wearing a bathrobe and a beret.

"*Bonjour, Maman.* Guess how I'm going to get an A in French?" I greeted her. Without waiting for an answer, I said, "I'm going to practice. Every Sunday I'm going to speak only French."

"What an interesting idea," Mom said. She swallowed some bagel. "But I don't know French. We won't be able to communicate."

Out went my lower lip, French-style. "Ah, *quel* shame. But *français* is important, *non?* All my schoolwork is so important, *Maman.*"

"Of course. But . . ." Mom put her pencil down and leaned toward me, folding her hands on her knees. "Sweetheart, I thought maybe this afternoon you and I could stop working and have some fun at a movie or . . ."

I interrupted her. "I have to go to the Metropolitan Museum today, to research a class project on the French impressionists."

Standing up, Mom said, "I'll go with you."

I wanted to say "Hurrah!" but instead held up my hand. *"Non, Maman, non.* Then it would be *jolie*—fun. I have to work." I smiled. "Even though you don't understand French, I know you understand that."

Mom stared at me for a minute, then said stiffly, "Indeed I do."

She was upset, and I was both sad and glad about it. Good thing I was meeting Heracles at the museum. I really needed to talk to him.

# 25

Sunny and warm, with a little breeze, it was a perfect spring day. People were sitting all over the wide steps that lead to the Metropolitan. Some were talking to each other, others raising their faces to get some sun, some watching a mime perform on the street by imitating people passing by.

Shoonck. As I took a picture of the mime, he pretended to take one of me with an imaginary camera, and people laughed.

Then Heracles ran up the steps, and I didn't see anybody but him. "Hey, it's great to see you," he said.

"You, too," I said.

"Did you tell her?" he asked.

At the same time I said, "Did you tell him?"

"I'm . . . I'm building up to it," Heracles said.

"I'm working on it," I said. I sighed. "But I don't like

turning Mom's world upside down, Heracles. Maybe
. . . maybe we should forget the whole thing."

"Uh-uh," Heracles said, looking right at me. "You
should be what you want to be—a photographer."

I looked in his beautiful eyes. "And you should be a
scientist."

"If you keep trying, I will," Heracles said.

"Okay, then. I'll try even harder," I said.

"Yeah!" He lifted my arms up as if I were a champion.
All of a sudden there was a lot of laughter and ap-
plause. Startled, Heracles and I looked around. Right
behind Heracles, the mime was lifting his own arms and
opening his mouth in a silent hurrah.

The next day was my sixteenth birthday. When I woke,
I heard Mom showering. Afterward she went to her
room, but from there she didn't go off to work. I figured
maybe she was doing something in her room that had to
do with my birthday. So I sneaked out of the apartment,
leaving on my pillow a neatly typed note:

> Memo
> To: Mom
> From: Alexandra.
> Have to get to school really early and leave
> really late today. See you tomorrow.

I hated to do it, but I had to.

After school Dana, Brooke, and Nell took me out for a
birthday pizza, which was a complete surprise. So was the
subscription to a photography magazine they'd chipped
in to get me. We hung out until one by one they went
home for dinner, then I wandered around taking pictures until it got dark.

Walking past the deli, I peeked in and saw Mr. Damaskinakis, Eleni, and Heracles. Even with Eleni there, Heracles ran out when he saw me. He handed me something—a paper plate with a pb&j, and a candle in the middle. "Happy birthday, Alexandra," he said.

"Just what I've always wanted," I said, laughing.

"There's another present, but it'll have to wait," he said.

"Heracles, did you . . . ?"

He shook his head. "Not yet. . . . You?"

"Soon," I said.

"Heracles!" his father yelled, and his girlfriend echoed, "Heracles!"

When I walked into the apartment I was sure Mom was still at the office. Then, on the coffee table in the middle of the darkened room, I saw a big birthday cake illuminated by sixteen little candles. On one side of the cake was an envelope with my name in Dad's handwriting; on the other, an envelope with my name in Mom's handwriting.

"Happy birthday, sweetheart." Mom was in a shadow, on the sofa.

My voice was a whisper. "Thanks, Mom."

Her face, softened by candlelight, looked pretty and very tired. "I hope you don't mind that I'm giving you money instead of an attaché case," she said.

I swallowed hard. "Mom, we have to talk."

"A long talk," she said, nodding.

"Mom . . ."

"But tonight I have work to do. And I'm afraid I'll be busy for the rest of the workweek," she said.

"Saturday morning? Oh, I forgot, you run then."

"Run with me," she said. "I'll go at a pace that's good for you. We'll run and talk together."

Impossible, I thought. "Okay," I said. I made a wish, took a deep breath, and blew out all the candles.

# 26

On Saturday morning Mom loaned me a sweatsuit and running shoes. The sweats were super baggy, the shoes too tight. I swore this would be the last time I'd wear her hand-me-downs.

About two minutes after Mom and I started running, and before either of us said a word, she was ahead of me. "Keep up," she shouted. "I can't," I shouted back. Would she slow down, though? Sure, for two seconds. Then she ran ahead again. "Alexandra, you've been trying to tell me something," she yelled.

"Well . . ." I yelled to her.

"Yes?"

"Yes."

"Well . . . what?"

"What? . . . Well . . ." My throat hurt more than my feet. Mom was now yards ahead. I gave up, stopped, and just watched her. If she really wanted to hear what I had to say, I realized, she'd slow down. Then I realized that if I really wanted to talk to her, I had to catch her.

I ran, and kept running. She was so far ahead. I forced myself to run faster . . . faster . . . It was so hard to breathe. Inhale, exhale, inhale, exhale. I got a steady rhythm going, but then my thighs turned to jelly. Mom was crazy. How could she do this? And she was more than twenty years older than I. I made myself move faster. Sweat started pouring from me, my legs started hurting. There was a burning sensation from my throat to my chest. Faster faster faster, I pushed myself. I had to catch her. I had to tell her.

All of a sudden I was next to Mom. Her head jerked in my direction. From her expression you'd think she was hit in the head with a brick. Then she laughed. I couldn't help laughing too. Who'd have believed I could catch up with Mom?

Then I started pulling ahead, and farther ahead. I began feeling good. I felt as if I were flying. Turning my head, I saw Mom beaming, giving me the V sign. "Go, Alexandra!" she yelled.

Full speed, feeling weirdly terrific, I ran to my favorite part of the park, the Great Lawn. As usual, all kinds of people were there doing all kinds of things—sunbathing, playing ball, walking dogs. In a few seconds I saw a dozen photographs. If only I had my camera, I thought. I slowed down to watch a boy flying a bird-shaped kite.

"Alexandra, go!" Mom yelled.

Now a real bird was flying next to the imitation. What a picture! For a few seconds the bird and kite soared and swooped together.

"Sweetheart, why'd you stop?" Mom was panting and

patting me on the back. "You can really run. You can run better than I. You could . . . you should . . ."

The bird flew off in one direction, the kite in another. I turned to Mom, making myself look in her eyes. Funny, in this light her eyes looked green. I'd always thought they were gray, like mine. Then I spoke softly, my voice shaking a little. "It's not for me, Mom," I said. "I don't want to run. And I don't want to go to the Harvard Business School. I want to be an artist, a photographer."

Hands on her hips, still breathing heavily, Mom stared at me. "Don't you think you're too young to make that kind of decision?"

That made me laugh. "If I said I wanted to go to the Harvard Business School would you say I was too young?"

"Alexandra . . ."

"Okay, maybe I'm too young," I said. "Maybe I'm too young to know who I am, much less who or what I want to be."

Mom sighed with relief and wiped the sweat from her forehead with the back of her hand. "Exactly. I . . ."

"All I know is, I'm not you." My voice was still soft, but it wasn't shaking anymore. "I don't want your life, Mom. I don't want to be a workaholic."

Mom's hand remained on her forehead for several seconds. Then both hands slicked her hair behind her ears. "So you think I'm a workaholic."

I hesitated just a second. "Yeah, I do."

Mom sort of sank to the grass. She put her knees up, rested her arms on her knees and her face on her arms. "I had lunch with Diana yesterday and she said the same thing."

I didn't say anything. I sat beside Mom, stretching out

my legs. Mom picked a buttercup. "When I was little," she said, "*my* mother told me if you brushed a buttercup under your chin, and it left a yellow mark, you'd get married." She stared at the flower, but didn't bring it near her face or mine. "Alexandra, my mother was so smart and energetic, she could have done anything. She married at eighteen, though, and spent the rest of her life in the kitchen as a housewife and mother."

"She raised you," I said. "That was an accomplishment."

"Yes, but she never had the choice of whether she wanted to accomplish other things." Mom's voice sounded strained. "Even when I was a child, I knew I wanted a different life." She opened her fingers, and the buttercup fell to the grass. "Is my being a workaholic hurting you?"

"A little. I think it's hurting you much more."

Looking up at the New York City skyline rising above the lawn, Mom said, "Alexandra, what if I said I'd slow down enough so you weren't hurt . . . but I can only slow down somewhat? What if I said concentrating on my career is what I feel I must do right now—maybe not forever, but now?"

I looked at the grass. "I can't make you stop," I said.

Mom turned to me. "Alex . . ."

Meeting her eyes, I said, "But you can't make me start."

Mom opened her mouth, then closed it. We looked at each other for a long time. She seemed to be studying my face. Finally, she spoke. "You know, Alexandra, you've always seemed so mature. I guess I thought you were grown up, in a way, long ago." She paused. "But now you're really growing up."

"I really am."

"You know what I wish?" Mom said. "I wish my mother had lived long enough for you two to know each other." Suddenly her eyes brimmed with tears. She blinked them back, though. She didn't cry. Her voice was strong. "I love you, Alexandra. Whoever and whatever you grow up to be."

Now it was my turn to study Mom's face, to feel tears well up, but stop them. "You know what I wish? I wish I had my camera with me. I'd like to take your picture."

Mom's eyebrows and the corners of her mouth turned up. "How would you pose me?"

I thought about it, then smiled at her. "Your choice, Mom."

She smiled back. Getting up, she posed legs apart, fists on her hips. "How do you like me as Wonder Woman?"

I looked up at her. "Whoever you are, I love you, Mom." I jumped up, we hugged each other very hard—and let each other go.

"I'm going to run some more," Mom said, wiping her eyes. "It helps me think, and you've given me a lot to think about."

"I'm going home for my camera. See you tonight for dinner out."

Mom took a step away, then abruptly stopped and turned. "Alexandra, would you like us to stay home and have peanut butter and jelly sandwiches tonight?"

"That would be unbelievably wonderful."

"Wait," Mom said. "I saw cashew butter in the gourmet shop . . . and orange marmalade. And maybe we could have Scandinavian flatbread."

Unbelievable was definitely the word. I held my stomach with one arm and put the other around Mom's shoulder. "I appreciate the thought, Mom. But maybe we can find a restaurant with food from Nepal, in the Himalayas, where the specialty is yak."

She laughed. "Hmm . . . do you think they have yak quiche?"

"Sure—yak quiche, yak mousse. Or maybe we can find a Nova Scotian restaurant that has *moose* mousse."

Mom laughed, kissed me on the cheek, and ran off. Shoonck. I took an imaginary picture. Good thing it was imaginary because it was a blur. But it was Mom.

The sun was brilliant over the Great Lawn. Shoonck. Shoonck. Shoonck. I took imaginary pictures of a middle-aged couple holding hands, a little girl and boy playing catch with their father and mother, an old woman playing peekaboo with a baby.

Shoonck. A picture of the New York skyline. So many pictures, so many possibilities. I went home, picked up my camera, and headed for Damaskinakis's Deli.

# 27

"So, Heracles, I told my mother," I said. "Did you tell your father?"

On my way to the deli, I was practicing talking to Heracles. I moved to the right, took big steps, lowered my voice. "Yeah, I did, Alexandra. Everything's great now."

Back to the left . . . smaller steps . . . higher voice. "Good, but not great," I said. "Heracles, there's something I have to tell you."

"What?" the real Heracles asked, coming out of the deli.

I was so surprised I answered him. "There's no Osgood," I said. "The guy you thought was Osgood Podhurst the Third was really Tweed Thorpe the Fourth."

His mouth dropped open, then his eyebrows knitted

together. "Are you serious? Why didn't you tell me
Tweed Thorpe the Fourth wasn't Osgood Podhurst the
First?"

"The Third," I said.

"Tweed Thorpe the Third," Heracles said.

"Tweed Thorpe the Fourth. Osgood Podhurst the
Third."

"Whatever!" Heracles shouted. Who'd have believed
he could sound like his father?

"Actually, it's not Tweed, it's Reed," I said. "After I
started calling him by his right name, so did Nell,
Brooke, and Dana, and now everybody . . ."

"It's nuts," Heracles said. "It's totally weird."

I looked right into his big, beautiful, gold-brown eyes.
"Heracles, I made up a boyfriend because I was jealous
of your girlfriend."

Heracles just looked at me for a minute. Then he said,
"There's no girlfriend."

"What?"

"Not any more. Right after I told Papa I wanted to go
to Stanford and be a scientist, not work in the store, I
told Eleni I couldn't be her boyfriend anymore."

"Wow . . . you told her *and* your father?" I was grinning.

He nodded, starting to smile. "And you told your
mother?" I nodded too. "How'd she take it?"

"Pretty well. But how will your father run the deli
without you?"

"Look." Heracles turned toward the store. Through
the window, we saw Theo bagging an order—strawber-
ries in the bottom of the bag, then eggs, then a six-pack
of beer. Mr. Damaskinakis was biting his lip, but he

wasn't yelling at Theo, and he was letting him work instead of treating him like a baby.

"Papa even reminded Theo to take his medicine today," Heracles said. "He's trying to treat Theo the way the teachers say he should."

"Hey, kid, hurry up with my salami sandwich," a customer said. Theo headed for the cold cuts—on his skateboard. Mr. Damaskinakis opened his mouth wide. I closed my eyes. A second later, I shuddered at the sound of the crash, combined with Mr. Damaskinakis's scream.

"Yeah, well, it might take a while to work it all out," Heracles said.

When I opened my eyes, Heracles was handing me something. "Here's your other birthday present." It was a book—*The Family of Man*—photographs of all kinds of families from all over the world.

"How did you know I've loved this for a long time?" I asked.

"I just knew."

We smiled at each other. "Heracles, tomorrow, want to go on a picnic?"

"I'll bring the peanut butter," he said.

"I'll bring the bread and jelly."

"They're so good together," he said.

I said, "So much better together than alone."

We moved toward each other. Shoonck. That wasn't my camera, it was my heart. I wouldn't need a picture to remember this moment.